"You've Got Chocolate On You,"

Matt murmured. He reached over and skimmed a fingertip over the curve of her lip.

Flustered, Allison set down her cup of cocoa. She glanced over the table but found no napkin. In thoughtless provocation, she tried to lick the chocolate off with the tip of her tongue.

"Here, let me," Matt said huskily. His hands gently cradled her cheeks, and his mouth came down on hers with exquisite delicacy. Allison caught her breath as his tongue and lips removed all traces of the chocolate. Try as she might, she couldn't find the willpower to pull away.

Dear Reader:

Romance readers have been enthusiastic about Silhouette Special Editions for years. And that's not by accident: Special Editions were the first of their kind and continue to feature realistic stories with heightened romantic tension.

The longer stories, sophisticated style, greater sensual detail and variety that made Special Editions popular are the same elements that will make you want to read book after book.

We hope that you enjoy this Special Edition today, and will enjoy many more.

The Editors at Silhouette Books

BARBARA DAWSON SMITH
No
Regrets

Silhouette Special Edition

Published by Silhouette Books New York

America's Publisher of Contemporary Romance

SILHOUETTE BOOKS
300 E. 42nd St., New York, N.Y. 10017

Copyright © 1985 by Barbara Dawson Smith

Distributed by Pocket Books

ISBN: 0-373-09246-6

First Silhouette Books printing June 1985

10 9 8 7 6 5 4 3 2 1

America's Publisher of Contemporary Romance

Printed in the U.S.A.

BC91

BARBARA DAWSON SMITH
writes historical as well as contemporary fiction,
enjoying romance in any genre. Born and raised
in Michigan, she is married and now lives in
Houston, Texas. NO REGRETS won the Gold-
en Heart Award from Romance Writers of
America.

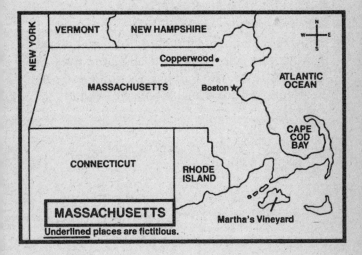

NEW YORK

VERMONT   NEW HAMPSHIRE

Copperwood

MASSACHUSETTS   Boston ★

ATLANTIC
OCEAN

CAPE
COD
BAY

CONNECTICUT   RHODE
ISLAND

MASSACHUSETTS

Underlined places are fictitious.

Martha's Vineyard

Chapter One

*W*hat if she slammed the door in his face?

Hands tightening on the truck's steering wheel, Matt forced that nagging thought from his mind. He slowed the Bronco to a snail's pace, leaning over to double-check the name on the mailbox alongside the winding country road. Off in the distance, through a scattering of winter-bare trees frosted with white, he caught a glimpse of a large gray clapboard house.

Impulse made him brake to a stop just after turning into the drive. Matt threw the gearshift into park and squinted pensively through the windshield. The midafternoon sun made diamonds wink and flash across the freshly fallen snow. Perhaps when she opened the door, her face would light up as radiantly as the blinding brilliance all around him.

His mouth twisted humorlessly. That hope might have sustained a dreamer, but not a man like himself whose life was ruled by stark reality rather than fantasy. So why had he even bothered to come here?

With slightly trembling fingers, Matt fumbled in the pocket of his opened sheepskin coat and pulled out a pack of cigarettes. He lit one to steady his nerves. He knew his question could be answered in one word. Obsession. Even after twelve years of trying, he couldn't get her out of his mind.

For a long moment, he sat back smoking, letting the warmth of the heater and his memories wash over him. He felt a curious sense of pride in the woman who lived in the house up ahead. Despite what had happened, she'd made a success of her life. For the hundredth time, he wondered if she had changed. Preparing himself for the worst, he tried to conjure up an image of plump thighs and sagging breasts. But it was no use. All his mind's eye could see was the girl-woman he'd been engaged to so long ago. At least he knew she hadn't married. He still had enough contacts in the nearby town of Copperwood, Massachusetts, to confirm that vital bit of information.

Frowning, he eyed the thin stream of smoke curling up from his cigarette. It had been years since he'd craved the tranquilizing effect of nicotine, years in which he'd calmly and coolly conducted board meetings, met with state senators and governors, and approved plans to spend millions of dollars. Now one small woman in this peaceful New England setting had him shaking like a schoolboy preparing to ask a girl out for the first time.

He wondered again if she'd slam the door on him without listening to what he had to say. There was only one way to find out. Matt took a final, comforting drag on the cigarette, then stubbed it out in the ashtray. Schooling his rugged features into the emotionless facade that had served him so well in the business world, he put the truck into gear and started slowly toward the house.

"One more and then I'm definitely going on a diet," Colleen said, selecting a chocolate-covered doughnut from the plate on the captain's table in the library. "Mmmm, this is heavenly. Why don't you have another?"

Allison O'Shea smiled fondly at her younger sister. Colleen had put on a few pounds over the past few years and was forever bemoaning that fact. Clad in the rose-colored uniform she wore as a waitress, Colleen was sprawled in the smoky-blue love seat opposite Allison, legs crossed, a foot swinging back and forth as she munched happily. She had stopped by for a quick chat before the evening shift.

"One's enough for me," Allison replied. "I had a late lunch so I'm not all that hungry."

"How come I didn't inherit some willpower, too?" Colleen wistfully eyed her sister's shapely figure. "I haven't fit into jeans that tiny since I was about fifteen."

"Now, come off it. You're hardly obese," Allison scoffed, taking a sip of coffee.

"That's what Joe used to tell me." The animation suddenly drained out of Colleen's face, diminishing the vitality that made her pretty despite a slight plumpness. She stopped just short of taking another bite, placing the half-eaten doughnut down on a napkin. "But I still can't help thinking that if I lost some weight, he'd come back to me."

"Colleen, you know your problems with Joe can't be solved so easily," Allison reminded her gently.

"I know," her sister moaned. "This whole mess is all my fault. I let myself go, I got too involved with the children, and I ignored Joe too much."

"It's not all your fault. Joe made some mistakes too. He could have tried to talk about the problem, but instead he just walked out and left you and the kids."

"He's been sending me money once a week. Oh, God, nine years of marriage down the tubes. Maybe I ought to eat myself into oblivion." Colleen stared balefully at the plate of doughnuts, but she didn't put her threat into action.

Allison sighed, absently tucking a strand of cinnamon-red hair behind her ear. How well she could understand what her sister was going through! A long time ago, she herself had experienced the same torment over a man. She wanted to reassure Colleen that the agony would gradually fade until one day it would be only a bad memory. But when her sister started blaming herself and defending the husband she'd been separated from for the past month, it was a sure sign that she wasn't going to listen to reason. The best Allison could hope to do was distract Colleen from her wretched thoughts.

"Hey, you want to hear something funny?"

"Thanks for trying, but I'm really not in the mood for jokes," Colleen said gloomily.

"This isn't a joke . . . maybe it's not even all that funny." Allison took a deep breath, then plunged in.

"Last week my syndication company sent me a licensing offer they'd received."

"A what? Oh, you mean . . ."

Allison nodded, encouraged by Colleen's flicker of interest. "You know, I get proposals all the time from companies who want to use my cartoon characters on mugs, calendars, greeting cards, whatever."

"My superstar sister," Colleen teased with a trace of envy. "Who would have dreamed when we were growing up that you'd be earning millions from a comic strip syndicated in 250 newspapers across the country?"

"Good Lord, I don't make even near that much! And it was only 238 newspapers at last count."

Colleen waved her hand. "Mere trifling details."

Allison breathed a prayer of thanks to see her sister's attention diverted. She hadn't intended to tell anyone about that licensing proposal, in fact she'd been trying diligently to put it out of her mind, but it was worth bringing up if it distracted Colleen. She realized that her fingers were clenching her coffee cup so hard they hurt. Deliberately she set the cup down on the table in front of her.

"Well, anyway, this latest offer was from a textile firm, and you'll never guess which one. Wakefield Mills."

"Wakefield? That name sounds familiar . . ." Colleen frowned, wrinkling her nose in the endearing way she'd done since childhood. Then concern flooded her face, and she sat up straight on the love seat. "Oh, Alli, that's Matt's company, isn't it? Did it upset you to see his name again?"

Allison lifted her shoulders in an indifferent

shrug. "He ended our engagement twelve years ago. Whatever feelings I once had for him are long since gone."

"But doesn't this mean that you'll have to work with him?"

"No, my contract with the syndication company gives me the right to reject any licensing offer. And you can be sure I turned this one down."

"I don't blame you. Oh, Alli, I don't see how you can be so nonchalant about it. I'd be a wreck if I ever got divorced from Joe and then ran into him again . . . knowing that he'd left me . . . that he didn't love me anymore . . ." Tears misted Colleen's green eyes, so like Allison's own.

Allison jumped up, thrusting a paper napkin into her sister's hand. "Don't cry, Colleen, please. Everything's going to work out for you, you'll see."

"But what if . . . if Joe doesn't want me back?"

"Then you'll make a life for yourself without him, just as I did without Matt."

"I don't know, Alli," her sister sniffed, wiping her eyes with the napkin. "I've never been as independent as you. I'm twenty-seven years old, and I've never been anything but a wife and mother."

Allison controlled a sudden surge of impatience. She didn't understand how women could let themselves get so dependent on men. "Listen, Colleen, you can learn to be independent. I know you can. And at least you have Jennifer and Lindsey."

"Yes, I do, don't I?" Colleen brightened at the mention of her eight-year-old twin daughters.

"And don't forget that you've got a job now, too. That means you're already starting to make it on your own."

"Oh, my Lord, the restaurant!" Colleen's eyes widened as she glanced down at her watch. "I'm supposed to be there by four-thirty on Fridays, and that only gives me ten minutes to make it!" She sprang up and dashed out into the hall, grabbing her coat from the closet. "Thanks for listening, Alli, but I've got to run. And thanks for the coffee and doughnuts—I'll return the favor sometime." She raced out the door, banging it shut behind her and leaving as her legacy a draft of frigid air from outside.

Allison smiled as she turned the dead-bolt lock. Would she ever get used to her sister's mercurial moods? Aside from a temper that matched the red highlights in her cinnamon-colored hair, she herself had far more control over her emotions. In fact, she had more control over her life in general. And it had nothing to do with her being two years older and wiser than Colleen. No, she owed it all to the bitter lesson she'd learned at the tender age of seventeen.

Allison walked back into the library, her moccasins making little scuffing sounds on the polished pine floor. She felt an intense rush of satisfaction as she looked over the symbol of her success, this room that doubled as her office. It was furnished with the country-style antiques she loved. Like the other rooms in the house, there was a fireplace to provide cozy warmth on cold winter nights. Beneath the matching pair of love seats she and her sister had occupied was a Bokhara rug in smoky blues and rich ruby reds. The faintly musty odor in the air came from the old books that lined the walls, including her collection of first editions.

Swiftly she cleared away the plate of doughnuts and the coffee mugs, dumping them in the kitchen before returning to the library. Though it was late afternoon, she decided there was still time to get some work done. Going to her drawing table, which was positioned perpendicular to one of the large multipaned windows, she picked up the black cat that was napping in the swivel chair and nestled the animal in her lap as she sat down.

"Go back to sleep, Esmerelda," she crooned.

Absently stroking the cat, Allison frowned down at the half-sketched cartoon taped to the flat surface in front of her. It just wasn't humorous, she admitted with a rueful twist of her lips. Thank goodness she still had a week left before the next batch of cartoons was due at the syndication company in New York! These past few days, her muse seemed to have skipped town. In fact, nothing had gone right since . . . but she wasn't going to think about that licensing offer.

Resolutely she lifted her green eyes to stare out the window. From here, facing the back of the house, she could see the old red barn with its lean-to shed. Behind it was a low stone fence, and beyond that, the gently rolling terrain was covered by a thicket of maples, oaks, and beeches. Their limbs were laden with last night's snowfall, the first major storm of the season.

Pride welled up inside Allison as she looked out over the pristine landscape. She owned ten acres of those woods, in addition to this house, which had survived more than two centuries of harsh New England winters. How she loved her home, each timber and nail! And she had earned every penny of the down payment herself. There had been no man around to pay the bills and, to be truthful, she preferred it that way. Her one close call with marriage had taught her that independence was a far more satisfying state.

So why, then, had she lately felt an emptiness deep inside her, an odd yearning for that special closeness between man and woman which she had known only once before, so long ago? And why couldn't she stop remembering? She was happy with her life, for heaven's sake!

Allison drummed impatient fingers on the drawing table, unable to prevent her brain from drifting in an annoyingly familiar pattern. Money. Men. Marriage. Matthew.

Matthew. Her fingers curled into a small fist that slammed down on the angled surface in front of her, waking Esmerelda. She gave the cat an absent-minded pat of apology. Why in damnation couldn't she stop thinking about Matt? She didn't like this vulnerable feeling of having so little control over her thoughts.

The nonchalance she had exhibited in front of Colleen had all been a front. Seeing the name Wakefield on that licensing offer had affected Allison more than she cared to admit. Twelve years had failed to dull the memories of gut-wrenching pain and the sickening sense of betrayal. Those wounds still festered, locked away in a corner of her heart. After the way he'd used her, how could Matt have the gall to think she'd even consider working with him?

Matthew Clayton Wakefield III. Even the name had the sound of old money, she reflected bitterly.

At one time, she hadn't been good enough for him. Was she more acceptable now that she had a healthy bank account? Or didn't it matter if he associated with her, so long as it was strictly business? Over her dead body she'd give his textile company the right to use her comic strip characters!

Allison's sense of humor returned momentarily as her attention shifted to the half-finished cartoon on her drawing table. Imagine "Kit & Kaboodle" on bedsheets! The heart of the popular comic strip was Kit, a young, single career woman with a streak of insecurity. Kaboodle, Kit's outspoken pet parrot, acted as both her conscience and nemesis. Kit didn't know if she wanted to get married. Stanley, her klutzy boyfriend, did want to marry. Kaboodle was always trying to break up the two of them because he hated Stanley's cat, which would come to live with them if Kit were to marry Stanley.

Allison grinned. She could almost see the design for those bedsheets now . . . there was Kit, fast asleep while hugging her teddy bear. Perched on Kit's shoulder would be Kaboodle, thinking: "Better teddy than Stanley and his cat."

A sudden draft of cold air from the window brought Allison back to reality with a start. Shivering, she rubbed the arms of her moss-green sweater, massaging away her goose bumps. Why was she letting that licensing offer upset her so much, anyway?

Most likely it had been dreamed up by some lackey designer at Wakefield Mills, and Matt was completely unaware of its existence. As the company's chief executive, he would have more important matters to deal with. In fact, it was probable that he didn't know, much less even care, about the success his ex-fiancée had made of her life.

Keeping that humbling thought in mind, Allison crumpled the half-finished cartoon into a ball and tossed it into an overflowing wastebasket. It was time to get back to earning a living. From the top of a nearby filing cabinet, she grabbed a clean sheet of paper. To prevent it from slipping while she worked, she taped the corners to the flat surface of the drawing table. She was reaching for her favorite mechanical pencil when the doorbell rang.

"Sorry, sweetie," Allison murmured to the black cat that snoozed in her lap. As she stood, she carefully placed Esmerelda on the cushioned seat. The cat yawned once and stretched before settling down to resume its nap.

The doorbell pealed again. "I'm coming," she muttered impatiently as she hurried toward the foyer. It must be Colleen. That old Datsun of hers was always giving her trouble.

Fumbling with the lock, Allison swung open the door. Her startled gaze met a strong masculine chin, then swiftly lifted to a pair of eyes in a unique shade of dark amber she had seen in only one man.

"Hello, Allison."

Her welcoming smile trickled away at the sound of that low-pitched voice. In stunned silence, she hugged the door. She felt trapped in suspended animation, a fly caught in the amber of his eyes. This couldn't be happening!

"Matt?" she whispered through numb lips.

His only answer was to incline his head slightly. Allison had a strange, fleeting impression of wariness in him that was quickly forgotten as her chaotic senses absorbed his familiar features, cataloging subtle changes.

Those faint lines fanning from the corners of his eyes hadn't been there twelve years ago. The grooves on either side of his mouth looked deeper and somehow sexier. His thick black hair still had an untamed appearance, though now it was more neatly trimmed, and a few strands of silver glinted here and there.

His hands were jammed in the pockets of his sheepskin coat, unbuttoned to expose a form-fitting white shirt. Time hadn't altered the wide breadth of his shoulders and chest, but she could see that his body was harder, more muscular. Now he had the taut physique of a mature man in his prime.

Again, his compelling eyes drew and held her attention. She decided that more than anything else it was the confidence he radiated that made him seem so different. A sudden, aching sadness welled up deep within her. The carefree boy she had once loved without restraint was gone forever. He had ceased to exist long ago, at the time of their heart-breaking final confrontation.

"May I come in?" Matt said abruptly. "It's damn cold out here."

For the first time, she noticed the icy breeze that whipped around them, tousling his hair and invading the warmth of the house. Allison shivered. What was he doing here? The reason hit her with meteoric force, tempting her to slam the door in his face. The licensing offer. She took a deep breath and marshaled her chaotic emotions. By God, she was no longer a naive seventeen-year-old! If he could handle the situation coolly, then so could she.

"I'm sorry. I didn't mean to make you stand outside in the cold. Please, come in." Allison stepped aside, watching him shake off the snow clinging to his expensive leather shoes. "You took me by surprise. I was expecting my sister."

"Oh? I hope I'm not interrupting anything."

"No, Colleen just left. I thought maybe she'd had trouble starting her car."

"So that's who was driving out as I pulled up. For a moment I was afraid I'd missed you."

Her heart skipped a beat as Matt entered, brushing against her ever so lightly. Allison forced a calm courtesy into her voice. "Let me take your coat."

She closed the door as he shrugged off his coat and handed it to her. She had to stifle a wild urge to bury her face in the warm, achingly familiar male scent that clung to the wool lining. Quickly she hung up the garment in the hall closet.

When she turned around, Matt was leaning against the door frame leading into the living room, one hand casually perched on his hip. He was watching her. His expression was guarded, but that wasn't all that was different about those amber eyes that had once held such tenderness. Now his gaze had a hard, seasoned quality, as though he had experienced much in thirty years of living. She swallowed, wishing he would get to the point of this unexpected visit, yet struggling with an insane desire to postpone that moment when he would walk out of her life again.

"So, how have you been?" she heard herself asking.

"Busy. It's taken a long time and a lot of hard work to get Wakefield Mills back in the black."

I'll bet it did, Allison thought bitterly. *It's too bad you weren't willing to put that kind of effort into our relationship.* Aloud, she said with studied politeness, "I hope things are better now."

"They are—in fact, this looks like it ought to be our most profitable year ever." He paused, his enigmatic eyes intent on her. When he spoke again, his voice was soft, caressing, disarming. "And how about yourself? I've heard rumors that you've done rather well."

"They're not rumors. I've achieved everything I've ever wanted."

"Everything?"

"Yes." But the firm affirmation sounded hollow to her ears. This was the moment she'd waited so many years for, to flaunt in his face the success she'd made of her life. So why did she feel so empty inside? She changed the subject. "I was sorry to hear about your father."

Matt shrugged, though a flash of sadness crossed his features. "It's been over three years since he died. My mother and I have adjusted. How's your family doing?"

"Everyone's fine. My brother Brian's married now. He and his wife just had their first child about a month ago."

"Really? It's hard to imagine that old rogue settling down and raising a family."

For the first time, Matt smiled, and the impact on Allison stunned her. She felt her stomach twist strangely. She had to check an impulse to reach out and touch him, to make sure this wasn't just a dream. Dear God, what was wrong with her?

"Look, why don't we go into the kitchen?" she

said abruptly. "I'll put a fresh pot of coffee on."
Wheeling sharply, she headed down the hall, bypassing the oak-banistered stairway that led to the second floor.

Matt followed close behind, aware of an enormous sensation of relief. The first hurdle had been overcome. When Allison had opened the door to him, he'd half-expected her to refuse him admittance. He wouldn't have blamed her if she had. After all, she had every right to despise him.

He studied the woman leading the way to the rear of the house. She had always moved gracefully, but now she had a poise, a confidence about her that he admired. Her jeans outlined a luscious figure that was still as trim as it had been in high school. Though he'd dated scores of women over the past decade, he'd never seen a sexier derriere. She was a delicious morsel of pure femininity.

His gaze trailed upward, eyes caressing what his hands longed to touch. She'd cut the thick, cinnamon-red hair that had once streamed to her waist. He liked the way it flowed softly to her shoulders now, with a mere wisp of bangs to emphasize those enormous deep-green eyes of hers.

Yes, he could see changes in her, but the mature woman she had become made her even more desirable. He knew what she looked like without those clothes, all creamy skin and ripe womanly curves. From the moment he'd walked in the door, he'd had to fight an almost overwhelming urge to draw her into his arms and kiss every inch of her.

Matt frowned, pondering her reaction to seeing him again after so many years. The polite, almost nonchalant way she was acting nagged at him. He'd been prepared to face sarcasm and hostility, the fury of a woman scorned. Why hadn't she given him a taste of that volatile Irish temper of hers?

A sudden sinking sensation wrenched his gut. Had the passage of time made her indifferent to him? His fingers itched for another cigarette, but he'd left the pack in his coat pocket. He could have dealt with hatred, but apathy? What would it take to fight that?

"Good-bye, good-bye. *Raawwkk!*" came a squawk familiar to Allison as they entered the kitchen.

"Do you mean 'hello,' or are you trying to get rid of us?" she scolded the parrot perched in an antique brass cage alongside the hearth.

The bird answered with a loud wolf whistle.

"Now that's more like it," she told him. Confidence flowed back into her, along with her usual sense of humor as Allison began to measure coffee grains into a coffee maker on the white tiled counter.

"The real-life Kaboodle?" Matt asked with a grin.

"Actually, his name is Mr. Screech. A fan of my comic strip gave him to me a couple of years ago." She threw Matt a wry smile over her shoulder. "I found out why soon after."

"Let me guess. He screeched more than he talked?"

She laughed. "Worse . . . he didn't talk at all. I've taught him all the words he knows, although he never seems to use the right ones at the right time."

"And who's this?"

Allison pivoted, holding two cups she'd just gotten down from the cabinet. Matt was sitting at the rough-hewn trestle table in front of the fireplace. A lanky hound was ecstatically nudging his head against Matt's hand, tail thumping on the brick floor.

"That's Winston," she said lightly. "Consider yourself honored. Usually he only rouses himself for meals and an occasional trip outside."

While the coffee perked, Allison plopped onto a rush-seated chair opposite Matt, who was busily administering a rubdown to Winston's ears. *See,* she lectured herself, *you can have a civilized conversation with your ex-fiancé. Matthew Wakefield means nothing to you. It was only the initial shock of seeing him again that made you feel so odd at first.*

"Nice house you have here."

Allison smiled. "I like it."

"How long have you lived here?"

Her eyes followed the movement of his hand over Winston's head. His long, lean fingers were sprinkled with black hairs. She remembered the delicious sensations they had aroused, stroking hungrily over her body. . . .

She dragged her mind back to the conversation. "What? Oh, about four years. I've really come to love this place. I've always wanted to live out in the country in an old house I could fix up."

She stopped herself just in time before launching into a proud description of how she'd single-handedly caulked all the windows, laid new tile in the bathroom, painted the kitchen cupboards. *Cool it, Allison. You're babbling. He couldn't care less about your piddly remodeling efforts.*

"Don't you ever get lonely living out here all by yourself?" Matt asked.

"My pets keep me company."

"But what about human companionship?"

"My family's just a few minutes away, in town."

"And men?" Matt persisted quietly. "Do you ever invite your boyfriend over?"

His dark gold eyes flowed over Allison like a physical caress. Instinctively she folded her arms across her breasts.

"I don't have a . . . That's none of your business," she amended quickly. She felt her confidence ebbing, and fought for control. "Excuse me, the coffee's ready."

She sprang up and darted over to the counter, her face hot. God, why she was acting like such an idiot? She poured the coffee, concentrating on keeping her hand steady. Her temper began to simmer as she automatically added cream and sugar to their cups. Who did Matt think he was, using that smoldering, sexy look on her, of all people? Did he hope to soften her up? If so, he had a big surprise coming!

She carried the mugs over to the table. Matt stopped petting Winston to take one from her. Any other time Allison would have laughed at the comical way the dog collapsed at Matt's feet, closing lazy eyes with a loud sigh of contentment.

"You remembered," Matt said, after taking a sip.

"Remembered what?" Allison managed calmly as she sat down. His deep, intimate tone had made her think of how he had once whispered endearments while he'd made love to her.

"That I like my coffee with lots of cream and just a touch of sugar."

He made it sound as though she must still be in love with him to have recalled that simple detail! He probably thought she'd spent the past twelve years mooning over him. The implication made Allison furious. It took every shred of her willpower to hang onto her temper and coax her lips into a polite smile.

"Why don't we forget all this small talk, Matt, and get to the point of your visit. I know why you're here."

"Do you?"

His dark eyes were suddenly unreadable. She had the oddest impression that he was on the edge of his chair, though he was sitting back casually, his large hands curled loosely around his coffee cup. She went on, not bothering to keep the sarcasm from her voice.

"It's no coincidence, is it, that just last week I rejected that proposal from your company? You want to use my comic strip characters; hence this unexpected visit."

"Ah, the licensing offer."

"What else?"

Matt shrugged. "So why did you refuse it?"

"I'm not obligated to explain my decision to you."

"But then how will I know what tactics to use to get you to change your mind?"

"Don't even bother trying," she said bluntly. "I won't do business with you no matter what you say."

"Suppose I were to sweeten the deal?" He leaned toward her, forearms propped on the table.

Allison watched the Oxford-cloth shirt stretch across his muscular torso. A patch of crisp black hair was nestled at the juncture of his opened collar. How well she knew the feel of that broad chest beneath her fingertips. It was all hard male flesh, warm and stimulating, strong and enticing.

". . . So what do you think?"

"What?" She looked up abruptly, realizing that Matt was speaking to her.

"I said," he repeated patiently, "how about if I were to double your royalty percentage?"

She shook her head in disbelief. "Surely you can't think that that would make me change my mind."

"Why not? Think of all the money you'd make."

The tenuous hold Allison had on her temper finally snapped. Good God, the nerve of him! Did he imagine he could buy anything he wanted?

"Money!" she spat out contemptuously. "That's all you've ever been concerned with, isn't it, Matt? Everything has a price—twelve years ago, getting me into bed cost you a marriage proposal. Then when you'd gotten what you wanted, you dumped me as fast as you could. You were afraid of what people might have said when they discovered your fiancée was from the wrong side of the tracks!"

She surged to her feet, fingers tightly wrapped around her coffee cup. She saw a fleeting expression that looked oddly like satisfaction pass over his features, but was too caught up in her fury to analyze it.

"Allison, listen—"

"I've had it with listening to you," she raged on. "The last time I did, look what it cost me! I'm not making any deals with a man like you. I don't trust you, and I never will!"

She slammed down her mug with a definitive thump, so that hot coffee sloshed over her fingers and onto the tabletop. "Damn!" she cried out, more from irritation than pain.

In a flash Matt was up out of his chair, hauling her over to the sink to run cold water on her hand.

Allison was acutely aware of his long, lean body pressing into her side. The subtle musky scent of his after-shave mingled with the faint, pungent aroma of tobacco. She felt her anger dissolve, though some strange turmoil still churned through her insides. She reached out with her free hand and turned off the faucet.

"I'm all right. The coffee wasn't really that hot. . . ."

She swiveled toward him as she spoke, only to find herself wedged between his body and the edge of the counter. Politeness dictated that he should back off now that he knew she wasn't hurt, but he failed to move. Instead he studied her lips with intent amber eyes. It hit her with the force of an explosion that he wanted to kiss her. She felt an instantaneous, unmistakable sexual stirring deep in her belly. It threw her into a panic.

"No," she whispered, her voice strained with alarm as she tried to wriggle free. She pushed against his shoulders, her hand leaving a damp imprint on his shirt. But she was pinned securely. All her frantic efforts accomplished was to make her more vividly aware of his powerful body.

"I'm glad you haven't lost that passionate Irish temper of yours," he murmured huskily, his knuckles brushing lightly over her cheek.

He bent his head nearer, stopping just short of her lips. Their eyes locked. Allison caught her breath, her limbs paralyzed with . . . what? Anticipation? She knew she should demand that he let her go. Her hands tightened on his shoulders but failed to obey the message telegraphed by her brain. He was so close she could discern every achingly familiar detail of his face . . . the deep gold eyes, the dark lashes, the chiseled mouth and nose. She recalled the texture of his cheek, slightly abrasive in late afternoon from the growth of his beard. She wanted to press her lips to his hard jaw. She felt her nipples grow taut inside the lacy confinement of her bra. Dear God, did his mouth still taste the same?

"Naughty boy, naughty boy," came a squawk from the direction of the hearth.

They sprang apart. A wry grin took shape on Matt's face as he glanced at the parrot hopping back and forth on his perch. "I see what you mean about that bird saying the wrong thing at the wrong time."

"On the contrary, for once his timing was right on target," Allison muttered.

She grabbed a dish towel and with furious strokes began to mop up the puddle of coffee on the table. How could she have even considered kissing Matt? It was just that it had been a long time since she'd been so close to a man, she assured herself. Any red-blooded male would have affected her that way under similar circumstances.

"You trying to wear a hole in that table?"

She realized that the spilled liquid had vanished. "I wanted to be sure the coffee didn't leave a stain," she said stiffly. "This table is an antique, and I don't want to ruin it."

"I see," said Matt, the ghost of a grin lingering on his lips.

Allison gritted her teeth, struggling to keep her cool. She thwacked the towel down on the countertop, pretending it was his face.

"Matthew, I don't think we have anything more to say to one another—"

"Whatever happened to Esmerelda?"

Allison blinked, taken back by the unexpected question. "Uh . . . she's still with me. I left her in my office a little while ago, sleeping on my chair."

"Can I see her?"

His eager smile made her heart lurch, reminding her of the eighteen-year-old boy she'd almost married. She found herself giving him a stiff nod. What could it hurt to let him stay just another few minutes to see the animal?

"Esme must be what, now? Twelve?" he asked as they walked across the hall to the library. "That's pretty old for a cat, isn't it?"

"Yes, and she's slowed down, but she still has her moments when she's as perky as a kitten."

They entered the spacious library and, after giving the room a cursory glance, Matt made a beeline for the swivel chair in front of the drawing table. He crouched down, dark brown slacks taut over his muscled thighs.

"Hello, old lady," he murmured, stroking the black cat curled up on the seat. Esmerelda lifted her head to sniff his hand, then licked it twice with her raspy tongue. Her purr was audible in the quiet room.

"Hey, I think she still knows me." He looked up. "Do you remember how we found her?"

Allison wanted to sink into the glow of his eyes. She swallowed hard before answering. "She was just a kitten. Someone had put her in a paper sack and left her alongside the road. We saw the bag while we were riding our bikes."

"And you heard her crying and stopped to investigate."

"Uh-huh," said Allison, her gaze soft with the memory. Matt had rescued the tiny creature and cradled it against his broad chest all the way home. That had been back at a time when she still believed in him, when she didn't know that his tenderness was just an illusion.

She stared down at his dark head, watching him scratch Esmerelda's ears. *Oh, Matt, how could you have seemed so sincere, so loving, and yet cast me aside? Didn't the vows we made that weekend we spent together mean anything to you? How could you have thrown it all away?*

Matt stood suddenly, scanning the love seats positioned on either side of the fireplace and the walls lined with books. "Are there any other pets hiding around here that I should know about?"

"Just some goldfish." Allison waved a hand toward a small glass tank sitting on a table. "Jaws One, Two, and Three."

He grinned faintly. "Doesn't Esme go after them?"

"Um, no, there's a screen over the top of the fishtank."

A long silence was broken only by a distant hum as the ancient furnace came on. They stared at each other. Matt was standing so close that she could reach out and touch him. But that hint of gentleness in his eyes was all an act, Allison told herself bitterly. She folded her arms across the moss-green wool of her sweater. How adept he was at playing on emotions and using people! He was here only because she had something of value to him. Damn him for raking up useless old memories in the process!

"Look, Matt," she said in her politest tone, "it's

been nice talking to you again, but I've got work I need to—"

"Why haven't you ever married?" he asked abruptly.

Allison started to retort, *because you taught me never to place my trust in a man.* She stifled that urge. She had to stop letting him get to her.

"I've got a successful career. What more could I want?"

"Children. Love. A real home."

"I have all that. Look at this house." She waved a hand around the room. "And I have several young nieces nearby to satisfy my maternal instincts, not to mention lots of other family and friends."

"That's not the same, and you know it."

No, you're wrong, wrong, wrong! Allison wanted to scream. Instead she gathered all her poise and said, "Look, if you're so gung ho on holy matrimony, why haven't *you* gotten married?"

"How do you know I haven't?"

She stared at him for a moment, transfixed. Never had she ever imagined his saying to another woman those same vows as he'd spoken to her that long-ago weekend at Martha's Vineyard. Her eyes darted to his left hand. No telltale gold band. But that didn't mean anything these days. Plenty of men didn't wear rings.

"Don't worry. I'm not married."

He sounded amused, as though she'd reacted exactly as he'd expected. No, not amused, but satisfied somehow.

"I wasn't worried," she snapped. "I was merely curious. In fact, if you want the truth, I was feeling pity for the poor woman you'd suckered into marrying you. I know from personal experience how meaningless a vow is to you."

"Don't be too sure about that," he said quietly.

"Oh?" she mocked. "What else am I supposed to think after the way you had your little fling, then broke up with me?"

She saw his knuckles turn white with tension as he gripped the back of the chair. Good. So he didn't enjoy being reminded that he'd treated her like a heartless bastard, did he?

"Allison, there are things you don't understand—"

"I suppose I should thank you for educating me," she broke in with a cold smile. "I was just a starry-eyed teenager until you told me you'd never really loved me, that you'd only been carried away by physical desire. I was too naive to know there were people in the world who played on emotions for selfish purposes."

"You've got this all wrong," he said urgently. "You don't know the whole story. I had my reasons for wanting to make sure you'd never call me and try to patch things up between us."

"Ah, so the truth finally comes out. You didn't want to take a chance that your low-class ex-fiancée might pop in and embarrass you in front of your high-society friends."

"Damn it, Allison, you're twisting things around." Matt raked a hand through his black hair. "It came as a complete shock when I found out that Wakefield Mills was on the verge of bankruptcy. I was no longer in a position to support a wife. So I did what I thought was best for both of us."

"Oh, yes, the family business. That was more important to you than our relationship, wasn't it?"

"For God's sake, I was only eighteen!" he exploded. "If I had to do it all over again, maybe I'd have acted differently. It just goes to prove that we weren't ready for a permanent commitment. We were both far too young."

"Isn't it strange how you came to that conclusion *after* we'd spent the weekend together," she taunted.

"Allison, please listen to me. I'd like for us to at least be friends—"

"Friends! After the way you . . ." She stopped and sighed heavily, massaging her forehead. "Look, I don't want to talk about this anymore. It's time you left."

"Not just yet. I had another reason for coming here—"

"Oh, yes," she inserted bitterly. "How could I have forgotten your scheme to use me again? You're wasting your time, though. I'm no longer a gullible teenager you can persuade to jump whenever you snap your fingers. You'll never see my signature on that licensing agreement. You might as well hop into your car and drive back to Boston right now."

"But that's what I'm trying to tell you," Matt said, with a glimmer of a sardonic smile. "I wanted to break the news to you myself. I'm not returning to Boston. I'm moving back here to Copperwood."

Chapter Two

*W*ith secret satisfaction, Matt watched the shock spread over Allison's face. Despite their argument, he had to admit that he was glad to see her blow her cool. It meant that she wasn't indifferent to him after all. Even hatred was preferable to the lukewarm reception she'd first given him.

"Bored with the big city?" she mocked finally. "Well, don't expect much in the way of an exciting social life in Copperwood. You lived here once—you should know that they roll up the sidewalks at eight o'clock."

He chuckled, though he knew she wasn't trying to be humorous. "I'll survive. After all, this is only a temporary move."

"Temporary?" It was no surprise to see her pounce on that word. "Why's that?"

"I'll only be here five or six months at the outside. I've decided to reopen the old mill."

"What? Oh, you mean that big brick building down by the river?"

"Exactly. I'm planning to personally oversee the renovation. I've rented an apartment in town for the duration."

His eyes followed Allison as she abruptly turned on her heel and went to the window to stare out. Matt felt a pang of guilt for stirring up what were clearly distasteful memories to her. For the umpteenth time, he longed for a cigarette. Denied that sedative, he concentrated on reminding himself that everything would work out for the best. It had to.

After a moment she swung back around and leaned against the windowsill. Her arms were folded across her breasts in a defensive gesture that brought back bittersweet reminders of the past. She had always crossed her arms like that whenever they'd argued.

"But why you?" Allison asked. "Surely the head of a company as large as yours wouldn't waste time on a job that could easily be delegated to someone else."

Matt forced a casual smile, sliding his hands into the pockets of his slacks. "Oh, I'll still be spending a few days a week at corporate headquarters in Boston. The reason I'm not letting anyone else handle this is that it's a pet project of mine. That mill has been in my family for over a hundred years. It was closed down about the time I was born, when Wakefield Mills, like a lot of other textile firms, built plants in the South to take advantage of cheaper labor."

"If it's not going to make you money, why are you doing it?"

"Because I'm convinced it can be profitable in the long run. We'll be starting on the interior plans next week. As soon as weather permits in the spring, we'll do any necessary exterior remodeling. Then we'll be ready for business."

Allison stared at him as though mulling over ways to get him to change his mind. Suddenly her expression hardened and she straightened up.

"All right, so you've done your duty in informing me that you're moving back to Copperwood. Now you can leave with a clear conscience. I'll get your coat." She started briskly toward the door.

"Allison, I meant it when I said I wanted us to be friends."

She stopped dead in her tracks and swiveled to face him, eyes glittering with a coldness that twisted his heart. "And I meant it when I said I'd never sign that licensing agreement. That's the real reason you want to hang around me, isn't it? So you can try to con me into giving you what you want."

"Forget about that damn licensing offer," Matt growled impatiently. Controlling an urge to grab her and shake her, he said in a low, persuasive voice, "Look, can't we just talk? We may as well face the fact that we'll be running into each other in town from time to time, so don't you think it'd be easier if we were friends? Let me take you out to dinner tonight. I'd like to explain why I had to break up with you. Things weren't exactly the way I led you to believe at the time."

He paused, watching her gaze at him with those big green eyes of hers, the fingers at her sides clenching and unclenching. Would he ever have the chance to make her understand that he'd had no choice?

He tried again, softly. "Please, Allison. All I want is to be your friend."

"Liar!" she cried out in a strange, choked voice.

Abruptly she spun toward the door. But she didn't storm out as Matt expected. She just stood there, head bent, arms wrapped tightly around her middle. He saw a slight tremor in her shoulders. The realization that he'd pushed her to tears hit him with the force of a fist slamming into his gut.

With a low groan he sprang forward and pulled her into his arms. She felt small and fragile nestled within his embrace. Her haunting feminine fragrance enveloped him.

"Honey, don't cry, please don't cry," he whispered, burying his lips in her hair.

"I'm not crying!"

Allison wrenched herself from him. Her green eyes were brilliant and hard as emeralds, and she blinked furiously as if to prove the truth of her words. Hands on her hips, she thrust her chin up to stare him full in the face.

"Tears would be wasted on a callous bastard like you," she blazed. "This may come as a shock, Matt, but you can't wind me around your little finger anymore. What kind of fool do you think I am? I wouldn't be your friend if . . . if you got down on your hands and knees and begged! So get out of my house—right now!"

Allison spun sharply and stalked into the hall. Matt stood stock-still, hearing her rapid, angry footsteps scuff over the bare pine floor in the direction of the foyer. The vehemence of her attack had caught him off-guard. For that one brief instant when he'd held her against him, he was wrapped in a fantasy that had haunted his dreams for years. Time had melted away, and he was eighteen again, cradling in his arms the only girl he had ever loved.

He closed his eyes, trying to recapture the quixotic memory. But it was no use. She wasn't his girl anymore. She was a mature woman with a life of her own. And she hated him more than he'd imagined. Maybe it would have been better after all if she'd been indifferent to him. What the hell had he been thinking of, to come here?

Matt opened his eyes, his mouth twisting in grim determination. He would never have achieved outstanding success in the business world if he'd been the type to give up easily. He may have lost the battle, but he was damn sure going to win the war. He marched into the hall to see Allison emerge from a closet. She held his coat, and she flung it at him as he approached.

"It's been wonderful seeing you again," she said acidly.

"The pleasure was all mine," Matt replied smoothly. As he strode toward the door, he threw on the sheepskin coat without bothering to button it. Grasping the doorknob, he pivoted to face her again, a faint smile flickering on his lips. "I take it this means you'd rather not have dinner with me tonight."

"Not tonight or ever," she forced out through gritted teeth.

"We'll see about that. I'll be back."

"Don't waste your precious time. I won't let you in."

But Allison's scathing retort was lost in a whoosh of cold air as the door slammed shut in her face. She leaned her forehead against the solid oak frame, trying to get her blood pressure down to a safe level. It was difficult, what with images of Matt pressing in on her. How could he have expected her to believe that song and dance about wanting to be her friend? She'd sooner invite a rattlesnake into her house!

Yet for one brief, horrifying moment back there in the library, she'd almost cried. *Cried*, for heaven's sake! It had been ages since she'd come so close to losing control. Damn him, damn him, damn him!

She took a deep, steadying breath. Shock sometimes did strange things to people, didn't it? It was the most rational explanation for that sudden, embarrassing sting of tears. She hadn't been mentally prepared to see Matt again after so many years. He had caught her off-balance, that was all. It wouldn't happen again.

With determined steps, Allison marched into the living room and curled into a kelly-green wingback chair. This bright, cheery room usually perked up her spirits. She had decorated it with an artist's eye for drama, using fabric and paint to echo the saffron, turquoise, and emerald in the antique kilim rug that covered the floor.

But today the vibrant decor did little for her. She stared pensively into the fireplace, its cold ashes the ebony color of Matt's hair. An image of his dark amber eyes persisted no matter how hard she tried to forget. . . .

At one time she had been gullible enough to take Matt at his word. She'd been seventeen when they'd first met, the summer before her senior year in high school. One day in June her older brother, Brian, brought home a new friend. Both boys had just started jobs as lifeguards at the community pool.

Tall, lean, and devilishly handsome, Matthew Wakefield was Brian's age, eighteen. Matt had just graduated from an exclusive prep school near Boston. While his parents vacationed in Europe, he was staying with his aunt in Copperwood. Allison learned that his parents had once lived in town, some years before she was born. The Wakefields were very wealthy and socially prominent in Boston, whereas she herself came from a working-class Irish background.

She had never been one to chase after boys, like all the other teenaged girls she knew. Such nonsense wasn't, in her opinion, as much fun as drawing on her sketch pad or dreaming about someday becoming a great artist. Yet she had fallen instantly in love with Matt.

That summer, the community pool became her hangout. She loved seeing Matt's tanned, muscled body sprawled in the lifeguard chair high above the water. He hadn't really needed the job because his parents were so rich, but he was working for the sheer enjoyment of it. Or at least, he teased, he'd planned on doing some serious girl-watching before he'd met Allison. The opportunities were abundant. Girls would strut past him, trying to catch his attention, yet never once did she see his head turn to stare after them.

But the idyllic interlude was doomed to end when his parents returned home, and Matt left for his freshman year at Harvard.

From then on, their relationship was composed of stolen moments. As often as they could manage it, either Allison or Matt would stay the weekend with each other's family. Tension mounted in her when it was her turn to go to the Wakefields' stately, four-storied mansion on Beacon Hill. Matt was an only child, and she felt uncomfortable around his reserved mother and father, so much the opposite of her own friendly, outgoing parents. Meals were stark and formal, and Allison worried constantly about using the wrong piece of silverware or spilling something on the pristine linen tablecloth.

When Matt suggested they sneak away for a few days to someplace where they could be alone, she swallowed her misgivings and agreed. Anything to be alone with Matt.

And so just before Thanksgiving Matt filched the key to the Wakefields' cottage on Martha's Vineyard. Her parents thought she was spending the weekend with his, and vice versa. Instead, she and Matt rode the ferry across the gray, choppy waters to the island where his family often spent their summers at a two-story house of white clapboard.

The beach was deserted. Though gusts of chill wind whipped at their clothing, they strolled along the sand, too wrapped up in each other to notice the cold. Only when the sun set did they finally go inside. Matt built a fire in the stone hearth, and they warmed their freezing fingers. Laughing and talking, they prepared their own Thanksgiving feast—

sandwiches washed down with a bottle of red wine Matt found in a cupboard.

Afterward, they sprawled on pillows before the snapping flames. Allison tucked her face into the crook of his neck, breathing in his male fragrance, giddy with happiness and wine. She was molded to his long, lean side, her hand resting on the sweater that covered his chest.

She murmured aloud the words that flowed straight from her heart. "I love you, Matt."

"Allison." Her name was a tender sigh, his warm breath fluttering against her lips as he pressed her against the pillows. His eyes were dark amber in the fireglow. She was aware of something different in the air, an electric charge that hadn't been present a moment before.

Their mouths met with the inevitability of fate. The touch of his tongue seduced her senses, sparking in her that familiar throbbing excitement only he could arouse. Flames flowed through her veins. Her palms flattened over his back to urge him closer, to somehow satisfy the growing ache inside her.

"Oh, God, I want you!" Matt whispered hoarsely, his fingers sliding beneath her lavender sweater to cradle her breast. "Please, Allison, let me make love to you."

She was tempted. Oh, to follow the natural instincts of her body, to learn the secrets of intimacy! Yet Allison had never been able to take the step. Matt saw nothing wrong with physically expressing their love for each other without the benefit of marriage. But she couldn't bring herself to accept his attitude.

"Matt, we can't," she forced out, shaking her head. "You know I was raised to believe that sex belongs only in marriage. I just can't ignore the teachings of a lifetime."

He rolled off of her with a heavy sigh of frustration. For a long moment he was silent, and she was afraid that he was angry at her. She bit her lip, fighting tears. Why did this have to happen to spoil their weekend together?

Suddenly Matt turned to her, resoluteness in his expression. "This situation is absurd," he pronounced. "Why don't we just get married now, instead of waiting?"

The unexpected proposal sapped her strength. "You can't be serious," she protested weakly.

"Oh, I can't, huh?" Matt got up and dug in the pocket of his jacket, then knelt beside her on the pillows. He held out his hand, and in his palm rested a ring, the large diamond solitaire winking in the firelight. "I bought this for you a few days ago," he said softly. "I had originally intended that we'd not get engaged until we both finished school, but why shouldn't we go ahead with our plans early? We can make all the arrangements next week."

Her heart warred with her common sense. "But . . . where would we live? And I was planning to go to college next year, too. How would we pay for all that?"

"We'll get a small apartment in Cambridge. Allison, I know how much it means to you to go to art school, and it means just as much to me. I've got some money set aside. We can do it. Besides, my parents will help us out with expenses."

But she wasn't convinced. She doubted the Wake-fields would be pleased to see their only son marry her. "I don't know—"

Matt drew her up so they were kneeling facing each other. "I don't ever want to be apart from you," he said, his voice husky. "You have my solemn vow that I'll love and cherish you every day for the rest of my life. Wear this ring as a pledge of my love." Lifting her hand, he slid the diamond onto her finger.

His eyes radiated the depths of his feelings. Emotion flooded her, washing away all of her misgivings. "Oh, Matt, I promise to be a good wife to you. I love you so very much."

They came together in a storm of need. Undressing each other with trembling fingers, they lay down before the fire. Caught up in the magic of his touch, Allison spread her hands over his muscled shoulders, shivering with excitement as he poured kisses over her bare breasts. Desire pulsed in her belly, more compelling than anything she had ever felt before. When he finally thrust into her, the jolt of pain was tiny in comparison to the fierce rush of love that enveloped her. She was his woman now, and no other man could ever claim her this way. With mounting urgency, their bodies surged together, plunging instinctively into that mindless abyss where nothing existed but sweet ecstasy.

For three glorious days, they couldn't get enough of each other. Matt introduced her to a wild rapture that she had never dreamed possible. Secure in his love, Allison was awash with happiness, even when they had to part late Sunday night. Brushing aside her offer to be with him when he broke the news to his parents, Matt said he'd arrange for her to join him in Boston as soon as possible. He made her promise not to tell anyone about their engagement until she heard from him, so she wore her diamond ring on a chain around her neck, hidden beneath her clothes.

But days passed and she didn't hear from him. Her calls weren't returned. Allison alternated between fury and fear that something had happened to him. She could think of no plausible excuse to persuade her parents to lend her the family car on a school day so she could go to Boston to see him.

Finally, on Saturday morning, he appeared on her doorstep. She'd been prepared to berate him for his neglect, but her anger quickly changed to concern. He looked as though he carried the weight of the world on his shoulders. His face was tired, and she sensed a remoteness in him that was different from his usual carefree nature.

When she threw her arms around him and tried to kiss him, he turned his head aside so that her lips landed on his cheek instead of his mouth.

"I've missed you so much," she exclaimed. "Where have you been? Why didn't you call?"

He ignored her questions. "I have something to tell you," he stated in a strange, abrupt voice. "Let's go out to my car so we can talk in private."

Puzzled, she got her coat, and they walked into the icy, drizzling rain. Allison sat quietly, waiting for Matt to speak, but he just stared out over the winter-bare lawn, his hands gripping the steering wheel. What was on his mind? she wondered. She had never seen him look so grim, so cold. Then he swiveled to face her, and she caught a flicker of deep anguish in his eyes before a curious blankness came down over his features. When he spoke, his voice was devoid of emotion.

"We can't see each other anymore."

She was sure she must have heard him wrong, and she cocked her head in numb bewilderment. "I don't understand."

"Getting engaged was a mistake," he stated bluntly. "I found out this past week that Wakefield Mills is in bad financial trouble. I can't afford to support a wife."

She felt a tremendous rush of relief. If money was the problem, it wasn't the end of the world.

"We wouldn't need much to live on, Matt. I can quit school and get a job—"

"No!" he exploded harshly. He added, his tone chilly and distant, "If you want the truth, money is only an excuse. I don't really want to marry you. What happened last weekend was a mistake—I guess I got carried away by physical desire."

Allison stared at him in disbelieving horror. "You can't really mean that."

"But I do."

His cold, quiet contempt cut to the core of her. Nausea swept over her in waves, and she could scarcely breathe for the stabbing pain in her chest. This had to be a nightmare! He was saying that he didn't love her!

"It's over between us," Matt continued without mercy. "I'm sorry if I hurt you."

He calmly lit a cigarette as if it mattered little to him that he'd just shattered her life into a million pieces. It registered through the agony ripping her apart that this was the first time she'd ever seen him smoke. It was somehow a symbol of the cold stranger he had suddenly become.

Somewhere in her devastation Allison found a fury unlike anything she had ever felt before. Arms wrapped protectively over her wounded heart, she lashed out in a blind attack.

"Your parents are behind all this, aren't they? I'll bet they were horrified when they found out their only son and heir wanted to marry a poor little nobody like me. They probably concocted that story of a business crisis to get you to dump me. And you weren't man enough to stand up to them."

Matt neither agreed with her wild accusation nor denied it. He merely sat staring out the windshield, smoking his cigarette, his face blank. Taut with misery, Allison realized she was seeing him through new eyes. It was like biting into a shiny red apple only to discover that the inside was riddled with worms.

"You know what, Matt?" she went on, her voice trembling. "You're no better than a robot. You'll never know what it's like to have real feelings, to love someone more than your own life." She stopped, struggling to contain her heaving sobs.

"Allison, I wish . . ."

His tone was low and strained, but she was too caught up in wretched despair to wonder why. She flinched as his hand hesitantly gripped her shoulder.

"Don't touch me," she choked out.

She jerked away and wrenched open the car door, running up the walk, her face streaked with tears and raindrops. That had been the last time she'd seen him until this afternoon.

For days afterward she had cried and cried until it

seemed every drop of emotion had been wrung from her. Her parents tried to comfort her and, desperately needing their support, she spilled out the whole story to them. As the shock passed, she realized how Matt had tricked her. That weekend together had been a charade. Knowing how she felt about premarital sex, he had planned things right down to the engagement ring, all to convince her to go to bed with him.

The knowledge hardened her heart. Slowly she began to pull together the shattered bits of her life. Proving to Matt that she was as good as his exalted family became her all-consuming goal. Someday, she vowed, he would see her living a life of luxury, and she would laugh in his face.

With passionate determination, Allison threw herself into her studies, winning a college scholarship. She concentrated on developing her artistic talent in an effort to achieve the success she craved. After graduating with highest honors, she landed a job with a prestigious New York advertising agency. Her hard work and long hours paid off in promotions and steady salary increases.

But she had problems dealing with men outside of the office. Her big green eyes and shapely figure gave her an illusion of fragility which drew masculine attention. But Allison accepted few dates. She was leery of men because most, she found, wanted sex in repayment for the price of a dinner.

Even when a man treated her with respect, she found she had no desire to pursue a physical relationship. It disturbed her that the heartstopping ecstasy she had experienced with Matt now eluded her. She finally was forced to conclude that she would never again love with such fervor. The emotional damage had created a stone wall around her heart.

Despite her success at the ad agency, she didn't feel fulfilled. She began to relieve her frustrations by doodling cartoons that spoofed her lonely, career-oriented life. At least the drawings made her laugh at herself. One night as she sat alone in her New York apartment giggling over the newspaper funnies, it suddenly dawned on her that she had the talent to develop a comic strip of her own.

Thus was "Kit & Kaboodle" born. With feverish intensity, Allison spent every evening and weekend for the next month creating two dozen sample strips. Then she popped them in the mail to a syndication company. To her astonishment, the syndicate called her within a week and offered her a contract.

Now, five years later, she had reached her goal. She'd moved back to Copperwood and bought this house and the surrounding land. At twenty-nine she had achieved a success that most people knew only in their dreams.

Yet with the passage of time her desire for revenge had faded in importance. She had quit fantasizing about what it would be like to run into Matt again, had stopped anticipating that imaginary scenario in which he groveled before her, begging her for a second chance. And there had been no reason to think she would see him again. His aunt, his last link with Copperwood, had died over ten years ago.

Allison drew in a long, deep breath. But now he was really and truly here. She might encounter him in the grocery store, the bank, the post office. Why did that make her feel so very vulnerable?

She stretched her cramped legs, rising from the chair in the living room. It seemed to her she had been sitting for hours, though dusk was just falling. To help get her emotions back on an even keel, she decided to do some work.

Heading into the library, she flicked on the light over her drawing table. Inspiration struck as she settled Esmerelda in her lap. After twenty minutes of concentrated effort, she tossed aside her mechanical pencil and grinned in wry delight at the rough sketch in front of her.

In the first frame, Kit and her boyfriend Stanley were on the couch, kissing passionately, while the parrot Kaboodle watched in disgust. The bird decided to do something before things got out of hand, so he squawked "Naughty girl," causing Kit and Stanley to spring apart. In the last frame, Kaboodle thought to himself in satisfaction, "A good guilt trip works every time."

Allison turned her eyes to the darkness outside, seeing only her reflection in the window glass, an isolated figure sitting alone in an island of light. An odd pang of desolation pierced her contentment, and her mind returned to Matt. Impatiently she brushed off the sensation of solitude. She wasn't lonely; she had her pets and her work to keep her busy. It was ridiculous, anyway, to associate Matt Wakefield with companionship. He was the most untrustworthy man she knew; that was why she had refused to give him the right to use her comic strip characters.

She frowned, absently petting the black cat snuggled in her lap. It was strange that the chief executive of a multi-million-dollar corporation would take the time to pursue such a minor matter as that licensing offer. It must be a game to him, she concluded. Matt wanted the cheap thrill of snapping his fingers and watching her jump. Undoubtedly it would be an ego trip for him to convince her to sign on the dotted line.

But the mistake he'd made was in believing she was still as malleable as she'd been at seventeen. He wasn't going to sweet-talk her into anything, not now that she knew what a manipulator he was. There was absolutely nothing he could say or do that would make her change her mind.

Chapter Three

$\mathcal{A}$lli, are you sure you don't mind watching the girls this afternoon since Mom's busy?" Colleen asked.

It was Saturday, and they stood in Allison's foyer. Her sister was on her way to work, and wore a coat over her waitress uniform. Allison was in jeans and a scarlet cowlneck sweater that rivaled the fiery highlights in her hair.

"You know I love having them here." Allison smiled down at her freckled, redheaded nieces, who were giggling and whispering to one another. "They're like my own kids."

"Okay, but I really hate imposing on you at the last minute like this," Colleen said apologetically. "If my boss hadn't called and practically begged me to work the lunchtime shift—"

"Aunt Alli, can we go see Winston?" Jennifer broke in.

"Please," their mother prompted.

"Yeah, please," Lindsey added eagerly in her twin's behalf. "And Esmerelda, too."

"Go ahead," Allison told them. "I don't know where the cat is, but Winston's probably in his usual spot in the kitchen."

"You two behave yourselves today, do you hear me?" Colleen called out as the girls ran down the hall.

"We will," they chimed in unison before disappearing through the kitchen door.

Colleen turned back to her sister. "I'm glad they left, because I wanted to tell you . . . Joe came into the restaurant last night."

"Did he?" Allison was instantly alert. "What did he have to say?"

"Well, for one, he was pretty surprised to see me there. He didn't know I'd gotten a job. I guess he thought I'd be sitting at home crying over him."

"See? Now you've shown him that you can be independent."

"I suppose," Colleen said, leaning a dejected shoulder against the front door. "The thing is, though, that I don't *want* to live without him. I like being married."

Allison bit her tongue to keep from saying, *even at the expense of your self-respect?* But this was her sister's problem, and Colleen would have to work it out for herself.

"Well, at least you've given Joe something to think about."

Colleen brightened. "We didn't have much time to talk because I was busy, but he did say that he misses me and the girls. He asked if we could have dinner together tomorrow night, after he takes Lindsey and Jennifer out for the day."

"I'm not complaining about watching the twins, but why didn't you ask Joe to take them today instead, since you have to work?"

"Well, I did consider doing that." Her sister's plump cheeks flushed. "But I've got tomorrow off, and I need to have enough time to fix lasagne—that's Joe's favorite meal."

Allison perched her hands on her hips in exasperation. "Why are you pampering that man? He's the one who left you. You should make him drive you into Boston and take you to the fanciest, most expensive restaurant he can find."

"I don't care about all that," Colleen said tearfully. "I don't need to be wined and dined. I just want him back." She fumbled in her purse for a tissue and, not finding one, wiped her eyes with her fingers.

Allison sighed and gave her a quick hug. "I'm sorry if I spoke sharply, Colleen. It's just that I want to see you happy again, and I'm worried you're setting yourself up for more hurt."

"I'll be all right. I know what I'm doing."

Allison frowned. "I hope so."

"Me, too." Colleen managed a smile. "Well, I guess I'd better get going." She opened the door, then wheeled back around. "Hey, I almost forgot. Who was that guy driving up as I left yesterday?"

Allison hesitated, then said slowly, "Believe it or not, Matt Wakefield."

"I thought it looked like him." Colleen closed the

door, staring at her sister. "But he lives in Boston, doesn't he? What was he doing here?"

Briefly Allison described Matt's plans to reopen the old textile mill, and also to get her to sign the licensing offer. She made it sound as if his visit to her was strictly business, leaving out the moment when she'd almost cried and he'd held her in his arms. It wouldn't serve any purpose to mention that, she reasoned, because it hadn't meant a thing and would never happen again.

"Do you suppose he wants to get back together with you?"

Allison recognized the gleam in Colleen's eyes. Her sister was an incurable romantic, and never gave up on her campaign to convince Allison to find a husband.

"Impossible," she stated firmly.

"But he came all this way to see you—"

"He came all this way to reopen a textile mill. It's just convenient for him to take care of another little piece of business while he's here."

"I still think it's got to be more than that if he took the time to drop by here personally."

"That's a moot point, because I have absolutely no interest in him. Now, aren't you going to be late for work?"

"Okay, I get the picture," Colleen teased as she opened the door. "If we don't want to ruin our friendship, we'd best stay out of each other's love lives."

Allison laughed. "Brilliant idea."

Her sister shivered as she stepped out into the icy air. "Brrr, it feels like January instead of November. Well, thanks again for taking the kids."

"Anytime. See you later."

Allison closed the door and sighed. Why did Colleen have to bring up that irritating encounter with Matt? Memories washed over her. She was in his arms, his experienced hands overpowering her senses. . . .

She shook her head as if to rid herself of her disturbing thoughts. Suddenly restless, she felt an urge to get out of the house. She hurried down the hall to the kitchen, a smile curving her lips as she entered the room. Winston was lolling on his side, tail thumping against the brick floor as Jennifer petted him. Lindsey was engaged in a valiant attempt to persuade a stubborn Mr. Screech to talk.

"Polly want a cracker?" said Lindsey hopefully, holding a saltine between the brass bars of his cage.

The brilliantly colored parrot regarded her with a baleful expression, then cackled something unintelligible and snatched the tidbit.

Allison laughed. "Hey, if I can drag you girls away from my pets, how would you like to go ice-skating out on the pond?"

"Yeah!" Both rushed over, Winston trailing along after them, his tail wagging furiously.

"Just the girls, Winston, not you," Allison teased. As if he understood, the dog ambled away to a rag rug in the corner, giving a mournful sigh as he pillowed his head on his large paws.

"We didn't bring our skates with us, though," Lindsey said. "We'll have to stop by home first."

"But we don't have a key," Jennifer pointed out. "I guess we could go to the restaurant and get Mom's."

"Let's not bother your mother," Allison suggested. "We'll just go to the skating rink in town instead, and you two can rent skates there. We'll save the pond for another time."

That decision made, Allison went down to the basement for her skates. As she returned to the kitchen, she heard a tiny scratching sound at the back door accompanied by a faint meow. She looked out the window to see a plump, gray-striped cat perched on the mat. The animal was a stray that had recently taken up residence in the barn.

"Why don't you two go wait out in the car for me while I feed Louisa," Allison told the twins. "I'll just be a minute."

"Can't we help you?" asked Lindsey.

"No. Louisa's shy around strangers. Here are the car keys," she added, rummaging in her purse and thrusting them into Jennifer's hand. "Now scoot."

After the girls grabbed their jackets and headed toward the front of the house, she opened the back door. Louisa padded inside, sniffing warily and keeping a cautious eye on Winston. The cat was in an advanced stage of pregnancy, and Allison worried about the kittens' being born out in that cold barn. But Louisa had resisted all efforts to coax her to stay in the house.

After feeding the cat and letting it outside again, Allison left through the front door. It was then that she noticed a beige Ford Bronco parked directly behind her silver-blue BMW. Jennifer and Lindsey were nowhere in sight. Allison frowned in concern as she hurried down the shoveled walk, skates swinging from one hand, purse in the other.

As she neared the drive, she heard the sound of deep, male tones followed by girlish laughter coming from the other side of the truck. Her breath puffed out in an irritated sigh that hung in the frosty air like a tiny cloud. Did that voice belong to the man she thought it did?

Her suspicions were confirmed a moment later as she threaded between the two vehicles to see Matt lounging against the cab of the truck. Her heartbeat accelerated—from intense annoyance, she assured herself. Today he was wearing jeans and a golden-brown crewneck sweater that matched his eyes. Despite the below-freezing temperature, his sheep-skin coat was unbuttoned. His bare hands were spread out wide as though to indicate great size, while the twins stood in front of him giggling into their matching blue mittens.

When he saw her, Matt dropped his arms. "Hi, Allison," he said cheerfully, as though their confrontation the previous day had never happened.

"Just what do you think you're doing?" she asked brusquely.

"Telling your nieces about the time I tried to squeeze two Great Danes into my truck. I was helping a friend get his dogs to the vet, and both of them wouldn't fit in the rear, so we were trying to put one in the back seat, but—"

"I'm not interested in your stories, Matt," Allison interrupted. "What I'd like to know is why you came here—" she paused, glancing over at two pairs of avidly interested young eyes "—after I specifically told you not to," she finished, swallowing the scathing words she'd wanted to let loose.

He grinned, unperturbed. "Well, I said I'd be back, and here I am."

"That's too bad, because the girls and I were just leaving."

"Oh, but Uncle Matt can go skating with us, can't you?" Lindsey asked, looking at him eagerly.

"Yeah, you'd like to go, wouldn't you, Uncle Matt?" Jennifer added her plea, an appealing smile lighting up her freckled face.

"Hold it just one minute," Allison broke in before he could answer. "First of all, Mr. Wakefield is not your uncle, and therefore you'll address him properly."

"But he told us we could call him that," Lindsey put in defensively. "He said he's a friend of yours, and that that makes him almost our uncle."

"Oh, really?" Fuming inwardly, Allison glared at Matt, who raised innocent eyebrows. "Well, I happen to disagree with him on that. And secondly, I'm sure Mr. Wakefield has far more important things to do today than go ice-skating." She shot him a warning glance, which he blithely ignored.

"No, as a matter of fact, I've got the whole day free. That's why I stopped by."

Allison's lips compressed, and her grip tightened on her purse and skates. Spending the afternoon in the company of this annoying man was not her idea of fun. Yet she sensed he wouldn't back down without a fight, and she didn't want the twins to witness that. It occurred to her that maybe it could work to her advantage if she didn't object. Considering the way she'd lost her cool yesterday, this was the perfect opportunity to show him how indifferent she really was to him. And, anyway, her nieces would be there to act as a buffer.

"Suit yourself, then," she said with a nonchalant shrug. "It doesn't matter one way or the other to me."

"Good. I'll drive," Matt said, taking charge. He opened the driver's door to let the twins scramble in. "You girls can sit in the back seat, and if your aunt will be patient a moment, I'll get the door on the other side for her."

"That isn't necessary. I can handle it myself."

Allison flounced past just as he stepped back to slam the door shut. When she veered sharply to avoid brushing against him, her heel hit a patch of ice. Her purse and skates swayed precariously as she fought for balance. In a flash she felt Matt's arms encircle her from behind, and instead of landing on the pavement she fell against his hard body.

"Hey, careful. We're not at the skating rink yet."

His deep, amused voice was so close she could feel the flutter of his warm breath on her face. A shiver raced over her skin, and she tensed her muscles to stop its devastating effect. She was, she reminded herself, supposed to be keeping her cool.

Seething inside, Allison pasted on a polite smile as Matt helped her into the truck. She folded her arms and gazed out the windshield, determined to ignore him. Yet as they headed into town her attention was drawn to the strong masculine hands gripping the steering wheel. Her eyes meandered in reluctant fascination over his taut thighs and flat stomach. Despite a cushy office job, he hadn't neglected physical fitness as did many other men his age.

"Something wrong?" Matt asked.

"What?" Startled, she saw him grin.

"From the way you were staring, I thought maybe I'd left my fly unzipped or something."

The twins giggled uproariously. Silently cursing the flush that crept over her cheeks, Allison stammered, "I was just wondering why you're driving a truck. I mean, it's not exactly your style. It's too . . ."

"Rugged?" he guessed, throwing her a teasing glance.

Allison started to explain that that wasn't the word she was searching for, then thought better of it. Despite his polished exterior, there was a primitive, pure male side to Matt. But if she said so, he'd probably take it as a compliment. She was in no mood to feed his ego.

"The point I was trying to make is that a truck isn't very sophisticated," she said stiffly. "Most corporate executives would choose something like a Mercedes or a Continental."

"Not if they have to drive over monster chuckholes every day. Until I can get the road out to the mill resurfaced, I'll be glad I bought this truck."

"Oh," she said grudgingly. "I hadn't thought of that."

Matt grinned. "Just to reassure you, though, I do have another car back in Boston. Would you consider a Ferrari expensive enough to suit my station in life?"

Allison gave a noncommittal shrug, determined not to be goaded into an inflammatory reply. She was silent for the rest of the short ride, holding herself aloof from the light banter Matt engaged in with the twins. When they reached the skating rink in the center of town, she hopped out, leaving the others to trail in her wake.

She gave Jennifer and Lindsey money to rent skates, politely declining Matt's offer to pay. While he hung up his coat on a nearby rack, Allison sat down on a wooden bench next to the locker where she'd stowed her purse. The twins perched beside her and eagerly pulled on their skates.

Lost in thought, Allison bent over to remove her shoes, sighing impatiently as she wrestled with one contrary lace. The knot in it annoyed her more than it would have any other day. Why did Matthew Wakefield have to invite himself along and spoil what could have been a very pleasant afternoon? Well, at least she could depend on her nieces to carry on the bulk of the conversation.

"We'll see you later, Aunt Alli."

Allison's head shot up as Lindsey's voice penetrated her thoughts. To her chagrin, she saw both girls wobble off on their skates, leaving her in sole charge of entertaining Matt.

"Hey, wait, you two!"

She bounced up, one shoe on and one off. But the twins were apparently chattering too much to hear her. She saw them wave excitedly to a friend they'd spotted on the other side of the rink, then join the crowd on the ice and glide off.

"They're Colleen's kids, aren't they?"

Allison spun around as Matt's voice came from behind. He held his rented black skates in one hand. She couldn't help but notice the way his golden-brown sweater clung to his broad chest. From somewhere deep within her came an impulse to reach out and touch him. *Ridiculous,* she scoffed silently. *You couldn't care less about this man.*

"What's it to you?" she snapped, irritation causing her to ignore her vow to hold her temper.

"I only wondered," he explained mildly. "You mentioned that your brother Brian just had his first baby recently, and Kevin is what now? Twenty-two or -three? That's a little young to have a couple of eight-year-olds. So by process of elimination, that leaves your sister."

"If you had it all figured out, why did you bother asking?" Allison plopped down in a huff and began to fiddle with the knot in her shoelace. Matt stepped over the bench and sat down beside her.

"Need some help?" he offered.

"I can handle it myself." She struggled for another moment, then impatiently tugged off the shoe with the knot still intact.

"You know, your sister's lucky to have two such nice kids."

Matt had picked up her shoe and was working on the knot. His pleasant manner suddenly made Allison ashamed of her snippiness. Why did she lose control so easily around him? Taking a deep breath, she tried to match his calm tone.

"Yes, she *is* lucky, isn't she? I only wish her husband felt the same way."

"Why do you say that?"

"A couple of weeks ago, Joe walked out on Colleen and the kids."

Matt pondered the information before answering. "That's not necessarily proof that he doesn't love his family. If he and Colleen were having problems, maybe they just needed some time apart. What does your sister have to say about it?"

"Oh, she claims everything is her fault for not paying enough attention to Joe. But I think the underlying problem is that neither of them were communicating with each other."

"What does her husband do for a living?"

"He owns a small construction company, Blair Building. But with the economy the way it is, Colleen says that business hasn't exactly been booming."

"So money could be a part of their problem, too," Matt mused. He tossed Allison's shoe onto the concrete floor, the knot in the lacing gone. "Have they tried to talk things over since he left?"

"They're having dinner together tomorrow night." At his interested look, she impulsively added, "Oh, Matt, she's so vulnerable. All Joe would have to do is crook his finger and she'd go right back to him."

"What's wrong with that, so long as they love one another?"

Allison stared fiercely at her stockinged feet. "She ought to have more pride. Don't get me wrong, I like Joe, but I'm afraid he'll take advantage of my sister's good nature just because the novelty of living as a bachelor has worn off."

"You don't know for sure that that's his motive," Matt pointed out. "Maybe he realizes he made a mistake. Maybe he's willing to work at saving their marriage."

She sent him an impatient glance. "Regardless, Colleen shouldn't let Joe just walk all over her like that. She's too dependent on him. Sometimes I think she ought to build a life of her own and forget about him."

"Like you did when we broke up?" Matt asked softly.

Her gaze locked with his. The odd mixture of tenderness and regret in his eyes touched her heart, and she tried to steel herself against him. But her pulses began to throb madly as she realized how close he was sitting. The noise from the crowded ice-skating rink faded under the assault of her other senses. She could feel the warmth radiating from his body and smell his musky male scent drifting through the cool air. She felt a peculiar urge to stroke his troubled features. Aghast at her weakness, she wrenched her gaze away, tightly curling her fingers around the edge of the bench.

"Yes, I *would* like to see Colleen become more independent, the way I had to," she said firmly. "Women shouldn't let themselves get so dependent. I don't need a man to make my life complete."

Matt's large hand came down gently over hers. "But why can't a woman be independent and have a relationship with a man, too? If we were friends, I wouldn't expect you to be dependent on me in any way."

Allison felt the slight thawing of her heart crystallize into ice again as she realized he had been manipulating her. What on earth had compelled her to confide in him her worries about Colleen? He hadn't really been interested; he'd been lulling her into a false sense of security in order to trick her into believing she could trust him.

She jerked her hand out from under his. "I know what you're up to, Matt, and it won't work."

"And I'm beginning to think you're afraid to be around me."

Allison gave a scornful laugh. "Afraid of you? Don't be absurd." She reached down and began to tug one of her skates over her stockinged foot. "I just wish you'd get it through your head that I won't change my mind about signing that licensing agreement."

"Fine," Matt said with remarkable calm as he began putting on his own skates. "So why don't we talk about us instead?"

"There is no us!"

"There was once. And if you'd listen, I'd like to explain something to you about our breakup."

"Why? I don't see any point in raking over old mistakes."

"Allison, please. This is very important to me." He stopped fastening his skates to frown at her.

For the first time that day, she sensed a crack in his cool composure. But it failed to give her any satisfaction. Allison stared out over the crowded rink, catching a glimpse of her nieces as they glided by, laughing. She had the strangest impression that she and Matt were enclosed in their own private bubble apart from the rest of the world. She didn't like that sensation one bit.

"Well, it's not important to me. I came here to skate, and that's exactly what I intend to do." Bending, she whipped back a strand of hair that tumbled into her face, then began lacing up her skates.

"Allison, at least listen to me."

She froze, feeling his fingers press urgently into the turquoise sleeve of her ski jacket. Though he wasn't touching her skin, her flesh reacted as if a phantom lover had caressed her, sending tiny goose bumps over her body.

"There's something you need to understand," Matt continued softly. "I want to be your friend because I'd like for us to get to know each other again. I realize now that I made a serious mistake when I broke up with you. I'll explain why if you'll just give me a chance."

The lace slipped out of her numb fingers as her brain focused on the words *get to know each other again.* He was casually suggesting they resume dating, as if his cruel rejection of her had never happened. An image flitted through her mind . . . for one bittersweet moment she was transported back to that long-ago weekend on Martha's Vineyard, his lips on hers, their naked bodies entwined.

Taking a tremulous breath, Allison buried the memory, seeking refuge in anger. This was just another ploy to use her. And even if he were serious, how could he believe she'd be willing to resume a relationship with the man who had destroyed her innocence?

"So I'm suddenly acceptable to you again, am I?" she mocked. "Is it because of my money? Or maybe being a cartoonist makes me a novelty. Are you planning on parading me in front of your high-society friends?"

Matt's fingers tightened on her arm. "That's ridiculous, and you know it."

"Then I was right," she said with biting hostility. "It *is* the licensing offer that's prompted this sudden interest in me. Well, it's too bad for you that I'm not fool enough to be swayed by a few sweet words of regret."

"Allison, you've got this all wrong. I know you must hate me, but—"

"I don't hate you. You're not worth the effort." She shook his hand off and bent to finish lacing her skates.

He went on in a low, rapid voice. "Allison, I lied when I told you I'd only been carried away by passion that weekend. I went to bed with you because I was in love with you. Don't you think if I'd have really tried, I could have convinced you to let me make love to you without going through the trouble of asking you to marry me?"

"Who knows or even cares?" She straightened up, stifling an insane impulse to believe him. "And anyway, you'd have no reason to lie like that."

"But I did," he said urgently. "Don't you see? I'd found out that my father's business was going bankrupt. My God, Allison, marriage would have meant you'd have to give up so much—art school, most importantly! How could I have asked you to do that for me? It had been your dream for so long. So I made up a story about how I'd used you. It was the only way I could think of to make you hate me enough so you'd stay away from me for good."

"Come on, Matt," Allison scoffed. "You can't expect me to swallow a wild story like that."

"It's the truth."

She flashed him a withering look. "Well, I don't believe it. I'd have been more than willing to live on beef stew instead of filet mignon. So why don't you just admit that it was your parents who pressured you into ending our engagement?"

He hesitated, running a hand over the back of his neck. "My mother was ill, and I didn't want to upset her—"

"So I was right, then," Allison interrupted. "Your mother was more important to you than your future wife."

Matt frowned at her, debating whether or not to pursue the issue. To an extent, Allison was right. His mother *had* forced him to end the engagement, but it hadn't been the way Allison had envisioned. Yet he couldn't bring himself to tell her what had happened. He decided it was safer to sidestep the issue for the moment. When—if—their relationship survived, then he would tell her the truth.

"Allison, we were far too young to understand what we were getting ourselves into. I admit I made a mistake. If I had it to do all over again, I know I'd handle things differently. Can't we leave it at that and concentrate on the future?"

"There isn't any future for us," she said stubbornly.

"Then how about the present? What do you say we call a truce just for the rest of this afternoon?"

"Matt, I really don't—"

His finger came down over her lips to silence her. "Surely a few hours wouldn't put too much of a strain on you. Please, say yes for old times' sake, if nothing else."

She wrestled with a strong impulse to give in. What did it matter if he was manipulating her? So long as she was aware of it, didn't that make her invulnerable? And in a way he was challenging her to prove that he no longer mattered to her. Pursing her lips, Allison nodded her head.

"Okay, truce—but just for today." She was oddly touched by the relief in his smile.

"Shake on it?" he asked, offering his hand.

"Isn't my word alone good enough?" she teased, though she slipped her fingers through his.

They moved toward the rink, laughing as they wobbled on the thin-bladed skates. When they reached the ice, Allison glided over the slick surface, reveling in the rush of cool air on her cheeks. She had loved skating ever since she'd gotten her first pair of double-runners at the age of five.

It was a moment before she realized that Matt was no longer at her side. Careful of the skaters streaming by, she turned to search for him. And there he was, right where they'd just gotten onto the ice . . . flat on his fanny and looking thoroughly disgusted with himself.

Stifling the amusement that quivered in her throat, Allison threaded back through the crowd to his side. He tried to get up, only to flop back down ungracefully. She could no longer contain the giggles that bubbled up, though she made a valiant attempt to hide them in the palm of her hand.

"What the hell's so funny?" Matt growled, looking utterly ridiculous with his long legs sprawled out in front of him.

"It's just that . . ." Allison paused to control her mirth, swiping at the tears that sprang to the corners of her eyes. "I never thought I'd see the chief executive of a multi-million-dollar corporation in such an undignified position."

"You might at least ask me if I'm all right," he grumbled. "I could have a broken leg, for all you know."

"Did you hurt yourself?" she asked in mock seriousness.

"No, but my butt's damn cold." He threw her a fierce glare, though a grin twitched his lips, and suddenly he started chuckling.

"Would you . . . like some help getting up?" Allison managed to get out between giggles.

"That's the least you could do after wounding my masculine pride by laughing at me."

"Poor baby," she said without sympathy.

Eyes still dancing with humor, she braced herself against the low wall that surrounded the rink and extended a hand to him. With her aid, he managed to scramble to his feet without further mishap. That accomplished, they both leaned against the wall, oblivious to the occasional glance directed at them by people whizzing past.

"When you said you'd go skating with us, Matt, I assumed you knew how," Allison scolded.

"I thought I did," he admitted sheepishly. "Of course, it's probably been twenty years since the last time I was out on the ice."

"You just need a little practice. Skating's like riding a bike . . . once you learn, you never lose the skill. Just watch me."

"Hmmm . . . I think I'm going to like this part."

He sent her a half-teasing leer, and the flame that lit his dark eyes could have melted ice. An unexpected physical response raced through her. Allison flushed, covering her confusion by pushing away from the wall to demonstrate a smooth glide. They stayed close to the edge, letting the other skaters pass them by while Matt imitated her movements. It wasn't long before he was cruising along with almost as much skill as Allison.

She found herself enjoying Matt's friendly banter as they skimmed over the ice. Warm from exertion and exhilaration, Allison unzipped her jacket to let the cool air flow over her. It was a wonderfully relaxing way to spend a Saturday afternoon, she decided, with a handsome man at her side, her cheeks glowing and her spirits high.

Wistful memories of the good times they'd shared washed over her. It seemed harmless enough to pretend for just a little while that they were teenagers again. She didn't object when Matt laced his strong fingers through hers. It was all part of the magic of the moment.

But time ticked along relentlessly, and soon she could see through the windows at the building entrance that the sun hung low in the winter sky. The next time she caught sight of her nieces, she called them over.

"We should be leaving soon," she told them.

"Aw, do we have to?" Lindsey objected.

"Can't we stay just a little bit longer?" Jennifer begged.

"Come on, Aunt Alli," Matt teased. "Be a sport. We're all having too much fun to go home."

Allison threw up her hands in defeat. Three against one was too much for her. Besides, she really didn't want this day to end either.

"All right, another few minutes, but then we'll have to go."

"Meet us in the snack bar," Matt added as the girls streaked off.

"Maybe I'd rather skate more," Allison teased.

"Have a little sympathy," he groaned. "This body of mine isn't as young as it used to be."

Grumbling good-naturedly, she let him tow her over to the locker area, where they put their shoes back on. Allison left her skates beneath a bench, planning on picking them up later. It seemed strange and yet so familiar to feel Matt's fingers splay over her back as they walked to the snack bar. There was something possessive in his touch, and she knew she ought to be wary of him. But the magic of the afternoon still lingered. Trapped in its spell, she didn't argue as he bought them paper cups of hot chocolate and settled her into the quiet privacy of a booth at the rear of the snack bar, sliding in along-side her.

She sipped at the steaming liquid, pretending an intense fascination with her drink to avoid looking at Matt. But though she managed an outward noncha-lance, she was intensely aware of the long legs stretched out beside her, the large hands curled around his cup, and the subtle odors of musky cologne and tobacco and something else, something acutely exciting that belonged to him alone.

She sensed him watching her, and slowly lifted her gaze. Her pulse leaped. How could his expression be so cool while his eyes were so warm?

"You've got chocolate on you," Matt murmured. He reached out and skimmed a fingertip over the curve of her lip.

Flustered, Allison set down her cup. She glanced over the table but found no napkin. In thoughtless provocation, she tried to lick the chocolate off with the tip of her tongue. Noticing his avid eyes following the movement, she averted her flushed face.

"Here, let me," Matt said huskily.

His hands gently cradled her cheeks, and his mouth came down on hers with exquisite delicacy. Allison caught her breath as his tongue and lips removed all traces of the chocolate. She sat in rigid silence, fighting a dangerous weakness in her limbs. But with slow inevitability, her bones were turning to water under his hypnotic touch. Try as she might, she couldn't find the willpower to pull away.

What's wrong with you? she asked herself. *You can't really be feeling this stirring of passion. He crushed that part of you long ago with his shattering rejection.*

Matt lifted his head to stare at her. She was appalled, swept with shame at the realization that she wanted him to go on touching her. No matter how much she tried to deny it, the shocking attraction was there. It was as real as the table in front of her.

"Allison," he muttered, running his fingers down her cheek to the pulse throbbing in her throat. "It's been hell living without you. I couldn't do it any longer. I had to come back. Please, let me into your life again."

She tensed, horrified by an impulsive urge to say yes, yes, yes! Dear God, what a mindless idiot she had been to trust Matthew Wakefield even for one afternoon! How could she have forgotten, even for a moment, the emotional trauma he had once put her through? Or his scheme for using her again? She propelled herself backward with a violent thrust, as though his touch were poison.

"You've got gall to suggest that—"

"Hi, Aunt Alli. Are we late?"

"Yeah, it took us a few extra minutes to turn in our skates."

The girlish voices of the twins stilled the scathing words Allison had been about to fling at Matt. Her nieces were gazing at her with curiosity from alongside the booth, and, with tremendous effort, she pulled herself together and smiled at them.

"No, you're not late. As a matter of fact, we're glad to see you two. Mr. Wakefield and I were just getting a little bored with each other's company, weren't we, Matt?"

The sweetness of her tone camouflaged the bite in her words from Jennifer and Lindsey. But when Allison glanced at Matt, she saw to her satisfaction that his lips were compressed tightly. He gave her an intent scrutiny before he slid out of the booth without answering.

The twins chattered all the way home, oblivious to the stony silence that reigned in the front seat. The truck hadn't even rolled to a stop in her driveway when Allison grabbed her purse, anxious to leave. But as she reached for the door handle, Matt's arm shot out in front of her.

"Give me the keys to your house," he commanded tersely.

"I'll do no such thing—"

"All right, then, I'll just have to get them myself." He lifted her purse from the seat between them and dug around inside. Then, as Allison stared in stunned amazement, he turned and handed the key ring to Jennifer. His harsh expression softened as he saw both girls watching him wide-eyed. "It's okay," he reassured them. "I need to talk to your aunt in private for a couple of minutes. You two go on inside."

"Don't you ever, *ever* order me around like that again," Allison snapped as the twins raced up the sidewalk. She wrapped her arms around her middle, fury bubbling up in her like red-hot lava. "I don't want to talk to you, not now or ever! I had a nice afternoon planned, skating with my nieces. . . ." Her hand flew to her mouth. "Oh, dammit, I left my skates at the rink. Well, that's one more thing I can chalk up to your account. If you hadn't made me so . . . so blazing mad by trying to put the make on me—" She stopped, too angry to continue.

Matt leaned back in his seat and fiddled with an empty package of cigarettes. "Are you denying that for a moment there you wanted me, too?" he asked, his mouth twisting in sarcasm.

"You're damn right, I am! This is a game to you, isn't it? All you want is to get me eating out of your hand so you can use me again."

"All I want is for us to get reacquainted," he insisted impatiently. "Don't expect me to give up that easily."

Allison gave a short, bitter laugh. "Yes, I guess the only thing you've ever given up on easily was our relationship."

Matt crumpled the cigarette package with sudden violence and flung it to the floor. He took a deep breath, and abruptly the anger drained from his face. He stared out the windshield, rubbing his forehead in a weary gesture that threatened to melt her heart. Another ploy, she told herself, hardening herself against him.

"Can't we just see if there's anything left of the feelings we once had for each other?" he said. "All I'm asking for is a little of your time."

"Oh, really?" she mocked, reaching for the door handle. "Well, I see no reason to pursue a dead relationship—especially one with a man who's incapable of caring for anyone but himself."

Through the gloomy interior, she saw him flinch. "Dammit, Allison, you've got to understand—"

She didn't hear the rest of his reply, because she whipped open the door and slammed it shut behind her. She stalked toward the house, head held high. But the pride that stiffened her spine deserted her once she was inside. She slumped against the foyer wall, feeling frozen, hearing the growl of Matt's truck fade into the distance as he drove away.

Allison took in a deep breath, striving for control. Why did he still have the power to devastate her senses? What had happened to her back there at the ice-skating rink? For a brief moment she had been ready to abandon herself to a man she despised.

She straightened her shoulders, telling herself in fierce determination that she would never allow that to happen again. Confidence began to trickle back into her. If there was one thing she'd learned in the long hard years since their breakup, it was that she had control over her emotions. No man could take that away from her. No man.

Not even one who had once owned her, body and soul.

Chapter Four

The blizzard came rushing down out of the north, darkening the afternoon sky to an eerie illusion of twilight. The icy wind howled like a banshee. Wailing its ghostly lament, it rattled windowpanes and hurled millions of tiny flakes into great, white drifts.

Snug within the warmth of her kitchen, Allison peered worriedly out into the storm. She barely noticed as a handful of snow pinged against the glass, tossed by a capricious gust of wind. Frowning, she pulled off her turquoise wool hat, then removed her ski jacket and threw the damp garments over a chair near the fireplace. Now what was she going to do?

She had just been out to the barn on a futile search for Louisa. When the stray cat had failed to show up for breakfast that morning, Allison hadn't been unduly alarmed. After all, Louisa came and went at will. But when the snow had begun to fall several hours ago and the animal was still missing, Allison had grown more and more concerned. What if the cat had gotten lost in the storm? Or even worse, what if she'd had her kittens, and they were all freezing outside somewhere?

The barn was the most logical place to search, since that was where Louisa usually stayed. But no matter how many times Allison called and no matter how many cubbyholes she inspected in the drafty structure, she could find no pregnant gray tabby.

After downing a reviving cup of hot coffee, she decided to continue the hunt inside the house on the theory that maybe the cat had slipped in unnoticed when the dog had gone in or out. But other than Esmerelda sleeping on a chair in the library, there was no cat in the basement or anywhere on the first floor. Allison was on her hands and knees looking under the bed in one of the spare rooms upstairs when she heard the distant peal of the doorbell.

As she hurried down the oak-banistered staircase, her mind still on the lost animal, she didn't stop to wonder who would be calling on her in the middle of a blizzard. She made a few cursory swipes at the dust clinging to her brown corduroys before opening the door.

A gust of swirling snow and frigid air preceded the tall man who burst in without waiting for an invitation. As she watched Matt slam the door, Allison was seized by a rush of gladness. Their conflict yesterday faded into insignificance compared to the pressing urgency of the moment. No matter how cavalierly he treated people, Matt shared her love for animals. He'd help her find Louisa.

He swung to face her, his hair tossed into disarray

by the wind and sparkled with melting snow. His wide shoulders were frosted with white, and for once his coat was buttoned.

"Why the hell didn't you answer your phone?" he snapped. "I've been trying to reach you for the past hour."

"Oh . . . I must have been outside when the phone rang."

"In this storm? You should know better than to venture out in weather like this when you're all alone here! Suppose you were to fall and hurt yourself?"

At the bite in his words, Allison felt a flash of resentment. "Who are you to tell me what to do? *You've* obviously gone out, so don't criticize *me.*"

Matt stared at her as he took several deep breaths, running a hand through his damp hair. The anger in his eyes changed to wariness, as if he half-expected to be kicked back out into the blizzard.

"I'm sorry for jumping on you like that," he said more mildly. "But when I couldn't reach you, I got worried. Maybe you'll accept these as a peace offering. Okay?"

She hadn't noticed her skates until he held them out to her. She had left them at the ice rink the day before. Her temper was mollified by the gesture of friendship.

"Thanks," Allison said, taking the skates from him. To hide an unexpected twinge of awkwardness, she added, "You look frozen. Could I interest you in a hot cup of coffee?"

"To be honest, I could drink a whole potful."

His smile deepened the grooves on either side of his mouth, making him look devastatingly handsome. The surge of physical response she felt was disconcerting. As they walked down the hall, she concentrated on calming her galloping pulse. She didn't have time to deal with sexual attraction. She—they—had to find Louisa.

In the kitchen Matt gave Winston a pat, then peeled off his coat and sat down at the trestle table in front of the fireplace. As he was drinking his coffee, Allison told him about the lost cat.

"I wouldn't be so concerned if I didn't know Louisa was about to have kittens," she finished.

"You're sure you searched everywhere out in the barn? A cat can pick some pretty strange spots to have her babies."

"Well, I checked all the likely places."

"Then we'll try the unlikely ones." Matt stood up and drained his cup, then threw his coat back on over his navy cashmere sweater. "Do you have a flashlight? It'll be dark inside the barn."

Allison got the flashlight out of a drawer and slipped it into a pocket of her ski jacket. Now that her despair at finding Louisa was lifting, she brushed aside the thought that she was independent and shouldn't need Matt's help; it felt good for once to have someone else to share the burden of worry.

She followed him out into the blizzard. The groaning wind whipped around them, threatening to sweep them off their feet. The icy gusts made it seem like Siberia instead of rural Massachusetts. With her mittened hands, she pulled her wool hat down tighter over her ears. The barn was a dark blur through the thickly falling snow. Several more inches had piled up in the short while since she'd gone out the first time. At least it was easier walking now, with Matt ahead of her blazing a trail through the deep drifts.

"Louisa. Where'd you come up with a name like that?" he asked as he struggled to shut the barn door against the storm.

"Her full name is Louisa May Alleycat. You'll never guess what I'm planning on calling the kittens."

He laughed. "I bet I can. You're going to name them after the characters in *Little Men* and *Little Women.*"

"Turkey. How'd you know that?"

"I know how your mind operates. Now let's find Louisa before we freeze to death."

Allison could barely see him through the gloom. By necessity they stuck close together, sharing the bright beacon of their lone flashlight as they searched up in the empty hayloft, in the dark cobwebby corners, and in the deserted stalls where Allison was someday going to stable a horse whenever she got around to learning how to ride. They even checked under the hood of her BMW, which she kept parked in the barn since there was no garage on the property.

"Can you think of anywhere else she might be?" Matt asked after they'd spent thirty minutes on the futile hunt.

Allison shook her head, rubbing her mittened hands together. Her teeth chattered from the cold in the drafty barn. "I looked all through the house. I can't imagine where she might have gone. Oh, Matt, suppose she's lost outside in the snow?"

He put his arm around her shoulders and hugged her close. "I'm sure she's okay. There're so many

nooks and crannies in this old barn. . . . Hey, I just
had a thought."

Allison lost his reassuring warmth as he strode off
toward the right side of the barn. Trailing along
behind, she saw him train the flashlight along the
base of the wall. Slowly the beam of light moved
over the snow that had sifted in through cracks in the
boards, then came to a stop at a space in the
weathered wood. Something was odd there, and in
an instant Allison realized what it was. There was no
snow blocking the hole.

"Isn't there a shed outside, on the other side of
this wall?" Matt asked.

Allison nodded. "Do you think Louisa could have
crawled into it from here?"

"There's only one way to find out."

He took her hand in his as they headed back into
the storm, keeping close to the side of the barn. The
wind seemed to have died down a little, though it
was still bitterly cold. Luckily, the tool shed was
unlocked. Using a shovel he'd brought from the
barn, Matt managed to dig away the drift blocking
the door so they could slip inside.

The flashlight beam roamed over a battered lawn-
mower, a ten-speed bicycle, and a general assort-
ment of junk. And there in the corner, nestled in a
cardboard box of old clothes, was Louisa. Curled
into her warm body were five tiny kittens with tightly
closed eyes.

"Oh, Matt," Allison exclaimed softly. "Look at
the little darlings!"

"Regardless of what mama cat thinks," Matt said
softly, "those kittens will have a better chance of
survival inside the house. Is there something we can

put over the top of the box to protect them from the snow while I carry them in?"

Allison found another box and rummaged around inside. "Turn that light over here, please. Thanks . . . I'd forgotten all about these old clothes I left out here. I do volunteer work for the community center, and I've been meaning to take these boxes in. How would this do?" She held up a pale-blue wraparound skirt for his inspection.

"Perfect," Matt said, taking it from her. "Say, this thing looks familiar. Wasn't this what you wore that time we drove to Cape Cod for dinner?"

"You must have an incredible memory."

"Actually, I recall being fascinated by the idea that all I had to do was untie the bow in the front, and the skirt would go sliding to the floor. Never got to test that theory, though."

Allison laughed. "Thank goodness we were with another couple that night."

"Ah, so you do remember," he teased, kneeling down on the cold dirt floor near the cats.

She didn't reply. It was better if he didn't know just how vivid those memories were.

"Careful, there," she cautioned. "Louisa's shy around strangers, and she's going to be doubly upset when we move her."

"She'll be good, won't you, honey? I won't hurt your babies, I promise."

Matt's voice was low and soothing as he spread the skirt securely over the box. Louisa mewed once, then all was quiet except for the storm sounds from outside.

"I'll run on ahead and get Winston out of the kitchen," Allison offered.

Matt nodded briefly as he stood up, clutching the box against him with infinite care. She held the shed door open to let him squeeze out. Then she hurried toward the house, head bent against the stinging needles of snow flung by fierce gusts of wind. Only a faint depression remained of their earlier path to the barn. Valiantly she fought her way through the large drifts, the lights in the windows ahead glimmering like ghostly beacons.

At the back porch, she stomped the snow from her boots and entered the house, leaving the door cracked open. She quickly shooed the dog out of the kitchen and closed the door to the hall. By the time she turned, Matt was already coming inside.

"Where do you want them?"

"Over here."

Allison indicated a spot against the wall, out of the path of traffic. He gently put the box down, pulling off the old faded skirt. Louisa sprang up with an indignant hiss and warily eyed her surroundings.

"We'd better leave her alone," Matt said softly, drawing Allison to a vantage point across the room. It seemed perfectly natural for him to slide an arm around her waist, and for her to lean into his snow-dampened coat.

"She'll be okay, won't she?" Allison whispered worriedly as she peeled off her mittens. "It's not supposed to be good to move a mother cat from the place where she gave birth."

"Well, she's still in the box the kittens were born in. We'll just have to wait and see if that satisfies her."

They watched as the gray-striped tabby cautiously sniffed the air. She was about to hop out of the box when one of the kittens made a faint mewing sound. Hesitating, she glanced around one more time, then lay down again to nurse her babies.

"See?" Matt said. "She's going to settle in here just fine."

Allison was about to reply when there was a loud *raawwkk* from the direction of the hearth. Before Mr. Screech could disturb Louisa, she hurried over to the parrot and quickly drew a cloth over his brass cage. "Hush up, you crazy bird," she scolded softly. "It's your bedtime, anyway."

Now that the crisis with the cats was over, she and Matt removed their coats. Allison tugged off her boots, her toes tingling as warmth returned to them.

She sank to her knees a few feet from the box and peered over the edge. "Look," she whispered, motioning Matt over. "Aren't they the most beautiful creatures you've ever seen?"

"Second only to you."

His soft words drew her head up sharply. The look of raw desire in his eyes as he knelt beside her threw her senses into a turmoil. His gaze meandered over her figure, lingering on the cream-colored sweater that outlined her breasts. Her skin felt suffused with heat. It seemed an eternity passed before he again met her eyes.

"I want to kiss you," he murmured, his voice rough with tenderness.

He touched her cheek with his hand. She'd be a fool to give in to the passion that flamed inside her, she thought dazedly. Yet, since her emotions weren't involved, what could there be in satisfying this sudden craving for one kiss? With a soft sigh of surrender, she swayed toward him.

Their mouths merged with mesmerizing magic. His arms closed around her with a fierce possessiveness that blended every pliant curve to his hard body. Opening her lips to his tongue, she forgot all but the wonder of tasting and touching him again. Mindless and trembling, she clung to him, fingers tangling in his snow-dampened hair. Nothing mattered but the exquisite sensations his hands and mouth were weaving.

She felt flushed with heat, the blizzard forgotten under the impact of the storm within her. The deep pounding of his heart echoed the throbbing in her own veins. His lips abandoned hers to seek the hollow of her throat, and she arched her neck to accommodate him. She was enveloped by his scent, a pure male essence which she had always loved.

His fingers glided down to her breasts, then lower still, over the slender indentation of her waist to the apex of her thighs. When he stroked her intimately, she exhaled softly, a compelling excitement surging through her body. Pleasure raced over her skin, and she felt more alive than she had in years.

"Allison, sweetheart," he whispered huskily, "let's go upstairs."

Feeling caught in a dream, she rose at the gentle urging of his hands. A stiffness from kneeling on the hard brick floor caused her to stumble slightly. Matt's arm came around her waist to steady her. There was something clamoring in her brain, but she couldn't seem to focus on what it was. For a moment he held her close, and she was aware of the strength of his embrace and, more dimly, of the power he held over her.

They were walking now, out into the hall, the

kitchen door shutting behind them. Arms entwined, they mounted the stairs. Through the uncurtained windows of her bedroom, she saw that snow was still falling. The wind moaned, rattling the glass panes. The shadowed room seemed cozy and intimate.

Matt flicked on the nightstand lamp. Its soft glow transformed the windows into mirrors that reflected the two of them standing beside the bed. Clinging to one of the posts for support, Allison watched him strip off his navy cashmere sweater, then begin to unbutton the pale-blue shirt beneath it.

The urgent litany inside her head became clearer. *You're crazy, crazy, crazy,* it went. *He only wants to use you; then he'll reject you as he did twelve years ago.*

Cold and cruel, reality penetrated the fog in her brain. Dear God, what was she doing? Passion drained away, leaving her body stiff and icy. Did she have so little control over herself that she would let him humiliate her this way again?

"Matt, no . . ." Her voice sounded appallingly weak, and she swallowed to ease the tightness in her throat before adding more firmly, "I'm not going to bed with you."

He strode over to her and seized her shoulders. "Why?" he demanded hoarsely. "Allison, I want you . . . I need you. We can be happy again if you'll just give our relationship a chance."

For one wild second she was tempted. Her fingers ached to touch the muscled chest exposed by his unbuttoned shirt. Then another chill swept over her, and her flesh crawled with goose bumps. She wrenched herself from his grasp.

"You only want to use me."

"That's not true," he insisted. "Allison, you must still have feelings for me. You wouldn't have come up here with me otherwise."

Her lips tightened. Was he suggesting that she was in love with him? "Don't delude yourself! Have you forgotten you taught me that physical desire has no connection whatsoever with emotion? Any man would have made me respond the same way!"

"I don't believe that for a minute."

"No? Then how about this one? If I have an affair, *I'll* choose the man, not the other way around. And you'd better believe you're at the bottom of my list of prospects!"

The narrowing of his eyes was the only indication that her barb had hit home. "You know, Allison," he said bitterly, "the problem with you is that you've become so damned independent you don't even have room for anyone else in your life. Maybe you're really afraid underneath all that coldness—afraid to make a commitment."

"Don't be absurd." Yet Allison felt a flicker of uncertainty, and lashed out blindly to deny his words. "It's the fact that I've succeeded without the help of you or your money that's really bugging you, isn't it, Matt? Admit it!"

When he didn't reply, she blazed on, "You'd just love to have me under your thumb again, wouldn't you? That's why you want me to sign that licensing agreement."

Ignoring her accusations, he began buttoning his shirt. "Don't you ever wish there was someone there to share your life with?" he probed. "Someone to confide your hopes and dreams in, someone to help you up when you're down?"

She averted her eyes. "I can take care of myself."

"Is that so?" Matt asked as he drew on his sweater. "Independence is wonderful until that inevitable day when you wake up and realize that you've never known the joys of having your own family. I only hope it doesn't happen to you after you're too old to do anything about it."

"Thanks for the philosophical advice," she said sarcastically.

"My pleasure." Matt strode to the bedroom door, then turned to face her. "Allison, I want you to know that I'll always be there if you need me."

"I needed you twelve years ago, not now."

She sensed that her bitter words had finally cracked his calm facade. Could it be that a spasm of pain had crossed his features? But all he said was, "You haven't seen the last of me."

He pivoted and headed into the hall. Sinking down onto the patchwork quilt covering her bed, Allison felt a rush of dismay sweep away her anger. How could she have come so close to sleeping with Matt? Damn this attraction she had to him! Why, oh why, couldn't the years have turned him into a balding, beer-bellied slob?

It was obvious that Matt intended to pursue her until he got what he wanted. Fury whipped through her again. What right had he to meddle in her life?

Allison jumped up and raced out into the hall. As she reached the top of the stairs, she saw him walking toward the front door, his coat and boots on. Winston was trotting along behind, wagging his tail, the traitor.

She leaned over the railing and yelled, "You stay

out of my life, Matthew Wakefield, do you hear me?"

"Anyone could hear you when you holler that loud." He flashed her a faint grin. "In fact, I wouldn't be surprised if your voice carried all the way into town."

Allison wasn't amused. "I mean it, Matt. I don't ever want to see you in this house again."

"Then I'll just have to make sure we run into each other elsewhere. Your dog wants out. Mind if I do the honors?"

"No, but—"

"Come on, Winston, let's go." Matt swung open the front door, shutting it behind them with a quiet click.

For an instant Allison stood speechless. Then she slammed her palm down on the railing, the slap of flesh against wood echoing through the empty hall. "I hope your truck gets stuck in the snow," she muttered childishly.

She wheeled around and stalked back into her bedroom to look out the window. The storm had died down, though the sky was still dim as twilight. Matt was shoveling away the drifts around his Bronco as Winston frolicked like a puppy. She smiled reluctantly. Snow was one of the few things that made her lazy hound lively.

She watched the scene pensively until Matt was inside the truck, warming the engine. After several false starts, the four-wheel-drive vehicle inched its way through the deep drifts, heading for the main road. She was glad to see him go, so why did she have this sudden stupid urge to cry? Allison pivoted, determined not to watch his departure any longer, but she found it impossible to stop thinking about Matt. Why had he talked of experiencing the joys of a family? Was it something he'd decided he wanted for himself? Perhaps he was planning on marrying soon.

Allison collapsed on a bentwood rocker, her legs suddenly weak. Did he have someone in mind? It stood to reason that a virile man like him would have lots of women in his life. Undoubtedly he would wed someone with polish and poise, someone with an ancestry that could be traced back to British nobility, a woman completely different from herself. Why did that depress her so?

In a wave of angry frustration, she stomped downstairs and let Winston back in, then checked on the kittens. For the remainder of the day she distracted herself by working.

To her amazement she was bursting with creativity. She decided to do a series of cartoons in which Kit's boyfriend Stanley goes on vacation, leaving his cat with Kit. When the cat has kittens, the parrot Kaboodle is horrified, and redoubles his efforts to keep Kit from marrying Stanley.

But as she sat at her drawing table late that night, Allison realized that she hadn't been able to purge Matt from her memory. Then one simple way to make sure he'd stay away from her for good popped into her mind. It was a desperation move, and it would mean swallowing her pride, but it was the only idea she could come up with.

The next time she saw him, she'd put her plan into action.

Chapter Five

*M*y dear, is something wrong?"

The voice took a moment to penetrate Allison's reverie. She'd been staring out the classroom window and into the night, haunted by the same memories of Matt that had plagued her for the past two days. But Mrs. Taylor's question abruptly brought Allison back to reality. They were at the town's community center, in a classroom which was normally used for teaching first aid, CPR, and other courses.

Allison turned her eyes to the tiny old woman who was gazing at her with curiosity. "What? Oh, nothing's wrong, Mrs. Taylor, really."

The white-haired woman looked suspicious. "Are you sure? For a minute there you were frowning so hard you looked like you were carrying the weight of the world on your shoulders."

"I'm fine; really, I am. I was just preoccupied . . . a little problem with my work. Nothing important."

"Now, Allison," Mrs. Taylor chided with irritating persistence, "I've known you since you were in diapers, and you can't fool me. What's really on your mind? Does it have anything to do with that Wakefield boy? I heard he was back in town, and I remembered how you two—"

"Hi, Alli. Hello, Mrs. Taylor."

Seeing Colleen thread her way through the boxes littering the classroom floor brought a relieved smile to Allison's face. Mrs. Taylor might look as non-threatening as a bit of dandelion fluff, but her appearance was deceptive. The elderly woman had a penchant for gossip, and could weasel it out of a person through sheer determination.

Colleen threw her coat on a chair, giving the room a quick once-over. "Looks like you two've got just about all the food in boxes."

The desks had been pushed aside, the empty space filled by large tables piled high with canned goods. The food had been donated by people in the community, and was to be distributed to the needy tomorrow, the day before Thanksgiving.

"Just about all that's left is the delivery," Allison told her sister.

"Joe offered to help with that," Colleen said. "He's got several trucks that he won't be needing tomorrow."

Mrs. Taylor's blue eyes lit up behind her wire-rim glasses. "Oh? Did Joe move back in with you and the girls, then?"

"Uh, well, not exactly . . ." Colleen floundered.

"Look, Mrs. Taylor, we're almost through here," Allison said quickly, diverting the woman's attention. "Colleen and I'll finish up. Wouldn't you like to go home and fix yourself a nice pot of tea and relax in front of the TV?"

"Oh, but I couldn't leave you—"

"Please, Mrs. Taylor," Colleen added. "You've done so many favors for us. Why don't you let us do just this one for you?"

"Well, if you insist . . ." the old woman said doubtfully.

"We do." Allison guided Mrs. Taylor's thin arms into a worn black coat. "If I don't see you tomorrow, have a nice Thanksgiving."

"You, too, the both of you. Such nice girls." Shaking her head, she pattered out of the classroom, gently closing the door behind her.

Allison looked at her sister, and they both burst out laughing. "Saved, thank God," she managed between giggles. "I wonder how long it'll take for her to realize she didn't learn a single tidbit of news from either of us?"

Colleen sank onto a nearby chair, convulsed with mirth. "Poor old Tattle Taylor. If it weren't for gossip I don't know what she'd do."

"You shouldn't call her that," Allison scolded, tempering her words with a smile. "She's a nice old lady, even if she did have me sweating just before you walked in."

"She was after you too? But why would . . . oh, you mean she'd heard something about you and Matt?"

Allison gave a hesitant nod.

"Say, what's going on between you and Matt, anyway?" When her sister didn't elaborate, Colleen went on gently, "Look, the girls told me he went skating with you guys on Saturday. And he called me during the storm on Sunday when you didn't answer your phone. So *something* must be going on."

"Nothing is!" Allison jammed her hands into the pockets of her jeans, pacing between two rows of boxes.

"Nothing, huh?" Colleen leaned back in the chair, eyeing her sister's restless steps. "Then why do you look so tense?"

"I'm not tense!" Allison threw her hands on her hips, glaring at Colleen. Then, with a heavy sigh, she sat down on the edge of a table. Maybe talking about it would give her a different perspective on the problem. "All right, I admit I'm a little uptight. It's just that I know Matt's using me, but I still can't seem to get him out of my mind."

"What makes you so sure he's using you?"

Allison quickly related her disagreement with him over the licensing offer. "And I haven't told you the worst part," she added gloomily. "I came so close to letting him stay overnight with me on Sunday—it really scared me."

"What's so bad about sleeping with him? You're both consenting adults."

"Maybe so, but there was a time when I needed a commitment first. And I was crazy in love with him back then! Now, knowing the way he uses people, why do I want to hop into bed with him?"

"Because you're a woman now, and you have physical needs. To tell you the truth, Alli, I think it would do you a world of good to have a man in your life. You're really missing out on a lot, not having that sort of close relationship."

Allison made an impatient gesture. "I'm doing perfectly fine all by myself. If I'd married Matt, I might have ended up . . ." She stopped, realizing what she had been about to say.

"You might have ended up like me?"

"Colleen, I didn't mean that the way it sounded," she hastened to explain.

Her sister gave a good-natured shrug. "Don't worry about it. Anyway, you're right. It's just lately that I've been able to see how bad it was for me to be so dependent on Joe."

"How was your dinner with him on Sunday?"

"Good. He ended up spending the whole day at the house because the weather was too bad for him to take the twins out. Then, after the kids went to bed, he stayed for a while."

"And?" Allison prompted.

"Well, for the first time in a long time we talked, really *talked*. He said he hadn't realized how important it was for me to have a job—not, of course, that working as a waitress is anything special, but at least I'm standing on my own two feet, and that makes me feel good about myself. And you know what? Joe said he understands that."

"I'm glad."

"I guess I should have been honest with him a long time ago, but I got hung up on being a perfect housewife because I thought that that was what Joe wanted. And now it turns out he doesn't care if there's a little dust on the furniture. He just wants me to be happy. It's amazing the things you can find out just by communicating."

"Does this mean the two of you are getting back together?"

Colleen hesitated. "Well, Joe says he loves me and wants to move back home, but I'm not sure yet. Everything's still so mixed up inside me—I want him but I want to try my wings a little, too. So we agreed to live apart for a while longer."

Thoughtfully Allison rubbed the sleeves of her bulky gray-tweed sweater, realizing she had underestimated her sister's strength. How wrong she'd been to assume that Colleen would jump back into the same old relationship!

"Are you sure you're happy with that arrangement?" she asked cautiously.

"Of course," Colleen said, stretching her legs out in front of her. "I'm having fun learning how to be independent . . . oh, I almost forgot! Take a good look at this—" she waved at her waitress uniform "—because it's the last time you'll see me wearing it. The reason I stopped by here was to tell you that I've been promoted to hostess! Jeanie's pregnant and her doctor ordered her to stay off her feet for a few months. Isn't it wonderful? For me, I mean, not for Jeanie."

"That *is* great news," Allison agreed with a smile.

"Well, I'm just now beginning to see that I missed out on a lot by getting married so young. This is my big chance to do something with my life."

"Don't say you haven't accomplished anything," Allison protested. "You've got two beautiful daughters and a husband who loves you. You should be proud of that." She realized to her surprise that in a way she was envious of Colleen, despite her sister's marital problems.

"Yeah, but I'll never have a wonderful career like you do," Colleen said wistfully. "And that reminds me—I got the December issue of *Woman's Life* in the mail today. You didn't tell me they'd done a feature article on you."

Allison shrugged. "The interview was so long ago, I'd forgotten about it." She leaned forward with an earnest frown, gripping the table edge. "Listen, Colleen, fame and fortune aren't the only things in this world that are important—"

The words died in her throat as the door opened abruptly and Matt walked in. Allison slid off the table and onto her feet, feeling her nerves spring to life. Dressed in a maroon flannel shirt and faded jeans beneath his unbuttoned coat, he might have been a construction worker rather than the polished executive she knew he was.

Matt walked a few steps into the classroom, his eyes locking with hers. Though his expression was closed, Allison sensed some deep emotion simmering just below the surface. She bit her lip nervously, wondering why she felt so panicked.

Seeing Allison's face, Colleen jumped up and hurried over to greet him. "Hi, Matt. Remember me? Alli's younger sister?"

"Of course . . . you're Colleen." He smiled, shaking her hand. "How could I forget the girl who used to spy on Allison and me while we were sitting on the front-porch swing?"

"I would never have dreamed of doing that!"

"Come on, now," Matt teased. "I saw you peek out the window a few times."

"Well . . . maybe once or twice," Colleen admitted.

Allison tuned out their banter, fighting a curious sensation of vulnerability. Why could this man, for whom she should feel nothing but contempt, make her pulse leap just by entering the room? She steeled herself against his magnetic attraction. This was her chance to get rid of him for good, even if the price was swallowing her pride. But just as she was gathering the shreds of her confidence, she heard Colleen asking him if he'd join the O'Sheas for Thanksgiving dinner.

"That's impossible!" Allison blurted out, startling herself with her vehemence. She stepped forward, quickly controlling her chaotic nerves. "What I mean is . . . Matt probably has plans to spend the holiday with his mother in Boston."

"No, as a matter of fact, mother's on vacation for a few weeks with some friends in Florida."

"Then you'll come?" Colleen repeated her offer, blithely ignoring Allison's murderous glare.

"Sure, I'd love to," Matt said.

"Great. Dinner'll be about five o'clock at my parents' house, but you're welcome to come earlier if you want," Colleen said, pulling on her coat. "I've got to go pick up the kids. See you guys later." She winked broadly at her sister before breezing out the door.

Matt turned to Allison with a sardonic expression. "You don't object if I accept your sister's invitation, do you?"

She bit off the stinging reply she wanted to utter. It would do no good to lose her temper. After what she had to say, she was sure he wouldn't show up for Thanksgiving dinner anyway.

"Suit yourself," she said with a shrug. "So what are you doing here at the community center? Certainly a man of your resources couldn't need a handout for the holidays."

Matt ignored her sarcasm. "I stopped by to drop off a check at the office . . . a donation from my company."

"Oh, really?" she said nastily. "And did you make your decision before or after you saw my car out in the parking lot? I can't help but wonder if this is an excuse to pester me."

He shot her an irritated look. "You've certainly got an exalted opinion of your own worth, don't you?"

To hide her sudden confusion, she walked to a nearby table and began loading cans of food into a box. Maybe it *was* egotistical to think that his whole life revolved around her. After all, he wasn't in love with her.

"Then how did you know I was here?" she asked.

"I passed this classroom on my way to the administrative office. I happened to glance in the door and saw you and Colleen. There was nothing covert about it."

"So, did you have something in particular you wanted to discuss with me?" She knew she was stalling, but couldn't yet bring herself to say what she had to.

"Yes." Matt hesitated, jamming his hands into his coat pockets. "I'd like to talk about Sunday night."

"What's the point?" she asked stiffly. "I almost made a stupid mistake. There's nothing more either of us can say about it."

"We need to discuss where our relationship goes from here."

Allison put down the can of green beans she was holding and folded her arms across her gray-tweed sweater. "I can tell you in a word where our relationship is going. *Nowhere.*"

They stared at each other. Matt's face was expressionless, and she wondered what he was thinking. It was hard for her to maintain an attitude of studied indifference when inside all she wanted was to throw herself into his arms. She steeled her shaky emotions with the reminder that he was only using her.

"I don't believe you really mean that," he said finally. "You can't deny that you feel something for me."

"Well, I do deny it," Allison retorted, hugging herself closer.

"Then why is this conversation making you so uptight?"

"It's not!"

"Your body language is saying something different, then. You always used to cross your arms whenever we argued—just like you're doing now."

"That doesn't mean anything." Flustered, she groped blindly for a can of food and put it into a box.

"Allison."

The soft, husky way he spoke her name sent a shiver down her spine. She gritted her teeth and ignored the delicious sensation, concentrating on the task in front of her. Hearing the faint scrape of his shoe, Allison glanced up to find him standing beside her. The intoxicating scent of his cologne filled the air, sparking all sorts of crazy urges to touch him, to lay her head on his broad shoulders. She couldn't move lest she succumb to impulse and make a fool of herself.

He reached out and gently pried a plastic sack of rice from her paralyzed fingers. "Can you finish this later, so we can go somewhere and talk?"

"I told you before, we have nothing to discuss."

Matt frowned. "Allison, we need to work this out—"

"I said *no!*" She took a deep breath to calm the sudden flare of temper before adding, "Look, there's no point in dragging out this charade. I know why you want to seduce me, what you're really after. So I've decided to let you have it."

He eyed her with sudden wariness. "What's that supposed to mean?"

"It means I've changed my mind about the licensing offer. I'll give your company the right to use my comic strip characters, since that's obviously the only way I can get you to leave me alone."

She leaned against the table to support her weak legs. There. She had done it. It should have been a relief to get it out, so why did she suddenly feel so desolate?

Matt continued to stare at her, his expression unreadable. "In other words, you think I tried to make love to you in the hopes of softening you up so you'd sign the agreement?"

"Why else?" Allison felt dangerously close to tears, and she managed to fend them off only by shoring up the eroding remnants of her pride. "This has been some sort of game to you, hasn't it, Matt? Well, you've won. Does that make you happy?"

Matt reached in his coat pocket and pulled out a package of cigarettes, lighting one. "You're pretty desperate to get rid of me, aren't you?" he asked tonelessly.

"I'll do whatever it takes," she said with forced lightness. "Just have your legal department mail me the contract, and I give you my word I'll sign it and send it back."

"No."

Allison swallowed. She'd prefer not to see him again, but if he wanted one more chance to gloat as part of the bargain, what choice did she have?

"Well, then, if you'd rather bring it over yourself—"

"That's not what I meant."

"I don't understand."

Matt blew out a thin stream of smoke. "I'm saying the deal's off."

"But why?" She cocked her head in bewilderment, feeling as though she was suddenly floundering in the depths of the ocean when she'd thought it was only a wading pool. "You can't change your mind like that."

"I just did."

"This isn't making any sense," she said, frowning. "Why did you try to seduce me, then?"

"That's an interesting question, isn't it?"

He threw the stub of his cigarette to the tiled floor and savagely ground it out beneath his foot. Then, without another word, he turned on his heel and stalked out the door.

Matt paused in the parking lot outside the community center, taking in great lungfuls of icy night air in an effort to ease the tension in his chest. It helped little. Noticing the curious glances of people entering and exiting the brick building, he strode the short distance to his truck. He whipped open the door, taking a small measure of satisfaction in loudly banging it shut behind him.

He put the key in the ignition, but made no move to start the engine. With brooding eyes, he scanned the parking lot. Lights were scattered here and there, shedding bright circles of illumination but leaving dense blocks of shadows elsewhere, such as the spot where he was parked.

His attention drifted across the street, to the people scurrying from store to store, taking advantage of the few minutes before closing time. The community center was located in the small downtown area of Copperwood, and from his vantage point he could see that Christmas decorations were already strung from light poles and traffic signals. The corners of his mouth lifted without humor. He wasn't in much of a holiday spirit tonight. To be accurate, he felt more like Ebeneezer Scrooge.

Oh, hell! Matt hit the steering wheel with his fist, unable to avoid his painful thoughts any longer. Why had he been so rash as to try to take Allison to bed? He had sensed that it was too soon, yet he'd gone ahead anyway. And look where it had gotten him. He had reinforced her opinion that he only wanted to use her. What a damn fool he had been, letting her go on believing he was serious about that licensing offer!

Maybe she was right about one thing. Maybe he *had* been manipulating her, though it wasn't in the way she thought. Maybe deep down he'd hoped that making love to her would convince her that she needed him. But now he could see how terribly wrong he'd been. Allison was no longer an easily swayed teenager. She was a mature woman, independent and with a mind of her own. It would take honesty, not subterfuge, to win her back.

Matt's mouth twisted grimly. That is, if he wasn't living a fantasy. Was it really possible that under those layers of defenses she might care for him? Or was he deluding himself because he was still in love with her after all these years?

He gritted his teeth against the hopelessness that threatened to engulf him. He wasn't one to throw in his hand just because the stakes were enormous and the odds were against him. He had to take the gamble. He had no other choice.

With fierce determination, Matt identified his number one priority. At the very next opportunity, they would have to talk things out. It was time Allison understood how he really felt about her and accepted his reasons for breaking their engagement. Except, of course, she wasn't yet ready to learn the role his mother had played in splitting them apart. What had happened had been his fault, and though he'd have to tell Allison about it sometime, it was better to wait until later. She resented his family enough already.

His second priority would be for he and Allison to get to know each other again as adults. He was beginning to see just how much they'd both changed over the past twelve years.

And if it killed him, their relationship would be

strictly platonic for the time being. It was obvious that sex would only make Allison more defensive. He couldn't take the risk of losing her forever in exchange for a few fleeting moments of paradise. He had to keep his hands off her.

Abruptly Matt tensed, seeing her walk down the steps of the community center and through the parking lot. No wonder he hadn't noticed her BMW. It was parked around a corner of the building, away from the main street, and was partially hidden by a large drift of snow.

As she opened the door and got in, a shaft of light from the overhead streetlamp made her cinnamon-red hair gleam with fire. She was a delicate woman, all cream and silk, but he knew the steel beneath that soft exterior. He told himself again that if he was ever to bind her to him, he'd have to be very careful. And because he needed her so desperately, he would do whatever it took to get her back, no matter how difficult it was.

While she warmed the engine, Matt turned his eyes to the large outdoor swimming pool just beyond her car. So many memories. The pool area was dark and deserted now, but at one time, that summer so long ago, it had been a place of magic for him and Allison.

Now, though, she was driving away without having noticed him. Somehow it seemed symbolic of their present relationship, but he was too tired to think about it anymore.

Seeing the BMW's taillights fade into the distance, Matt suddenly was aware of the cold night air seeping into his bones. Though it had been unconscious, he realized that he'd been waiting for her to come out of the building. And now that she was gone, there was no longer any reason to continue to sit out here in the frigid weather. He started the engine and pulled out of the parking lot, heading for the dubious comfort of his empty apartment and a good, stiff drink.

Chapter Six

Allison stood before the kitchen sink at her parents' house, the bodice of her peach sweater-dress swelling as she took in a deep, delicious breath. If there was one of the five senses she would always associate with Thanksgiving, she knew it would be smell. Other people might argue that taste was far more important, but not for her. It was the anticipation of it all, rather than the dinner itself, that she enjoyed the most.

Today the air was laden with marvelous scents. There was the spiciness of freshly baked pumpkin pie, the sweetness of candied yams, the succulence of roasting turkey, the tang of cranberry sauce.

A voice broke into Allison's reverie. "Colleen mentioned that she'd asked Matt Wakefield to dinner."

Allison glanced at her mother, a plump woman

with silvering dark hair. "Oh, yes, I'd almost forgotten." It was just a tiny white lie, she rationalized, using a peeler to attack the potato she held. In truth, she'd done little else but think of Matt since their encounter at the community center.

"Did it bother you to see him again?" Mrs. O'Shea asked.

"Why should it? There's nothing between us anymore. In fact, I doubt he'll even show up here today."

"Colleen said he'd accepted her invitation. What makes you think he won't come?"

"I . . . I just don't think he will, that's all," Allison hedged, not wanting to go into the details.

She felt a flash of confusion. Why had he changed his mind about the licensing offer? And if it wasn't her comic strip characters he was interested in, then why *had* he been pursuing her? Did he hope to have an affair with her while he was stuck in this small town? The thought made her insides quiver, a feeling which she firmly squelched. Now that he knew she would relinquish even her pride to get rid of him, she was sure he had finally realized that his efforts were futile.

"That's a shame he won't be here, then," said Mrs. O'Shea. "Your father and I were looking forward to seeing him again."

"You were?" Allison put down the potato, staring at her mother in surprise. "I thought you didn't like him."

"Why, of course we did. We wouldn't have allowed you to date a college boy if we didn't approve of him."

"I didn't mean you disliked him at first. I meant

afterward, when you found out about how he'd used me."

Mrs. O'Shea shrugged. "Honey, the both of you made a mistake rushing into things like that. But it's no reason for me to hate him now. And besides, what happened was a blessing in disguise. Neither of you was old enough to handle the responsibilities of marriage."

"I was almost eighteen," Allison objected.

Her mother laughed, picking up a stalk of celery. "That's still a baby."

"But Colleen was eighteen when she got married."

"Colleen was at least out of high school." Mrs. O'Shea sent her a thoughtful look. "You've always said you're happier being independent. Have you changed your mind about that?"

"No, of course not."

Why was she arguing, then? Allison wondered as she diced the potatoes. If she'd married Matt, she'd never have achieved success with the comic strip. She might have been a dependent, boring housewife with nothing more to talk about than her children. The thought made her shudder.

"Mom, have you ever regretted not having a career?" she asked impulsively.

"Raising you kids was enough of a career for me." Mrs. O'Shea smiled as she basted the turkey. "Though if you'd asked me that when I was thirty years old with four children age ten and under, maybe I'd have answered differently."

"How did you manage to keep your sanity?"

"I kept reminding myself how much I loved all of you," her mother said dryly. "It was hard occasionally, like the time you used your crayons to draw roads all over the living room walls."

"No one had ever told me not to do that," Allison pointed out with an impish grin. "I was just a budding artist following my creative urges."

The doorbell interrupted their conversation. "I'll get it," she offered, wiping her hands on a dish towel.

But her father already had the door open as Allison walked into the living room. A lanky man wearing wire-rim glasses, Mr. O'Shea looked more like a scholar than the high school athletic director he was.

She shivered from the cold that rushed inside as the newcomers entered the small living room. A doctor at the local hospital, her older brother Brian was tall and lean like his father, with dark russet hair. His wife, Susan, was carrying their infant daughter. Allison took the baby while Susan removed her coat.

"Hi, Heather," she murmured.

Wrapped in a blanket so that only her tiny face peeped out, Heather stared up with solemn blue eyes. A surge of intense longing left Allison feeling weak. How she wanted a baby of her own! More and more lately she had been aware of a desire to have children. Yet how could she reconcile this yearning with an equally strong need for independence?

The doorbell rang again, and her father answered the summons. The sound of a familiar deep voice made her head snap up in surprise.

It was Matt. Allison checked an impulse to raise a hand to her hair and make sure it was neat. Their eyes met briefly; then he turned to greet the others.

She calmed the wild beating of her heart, stifling her unexpected gladness. So he had come after all.

"I've been looking forward to seeing you again," Brian told him. "How long has it been since you were last in town? Must be ten years at least."

"Twelve, as a matter of fact," Matt replied. Mr. O'Shea took his topcoat and went to hang it up in the hall closet.

"Mom said something about your being here to build a new textile plant," Brian went on.

"Actually, it's not exactly new. I'm renovating the old mill down by the river."

"We were pleased to hear about that," Mr. O'Shea said as he returned to the living room. "It'll do a lot of good for the economy in Copperwood."

They discussed the mill for a moment. Then Matt turned to Brian and grinned. "Allison told me you'd gotten married. I can't believe this is the same guy who swore to me that he'd never give up his bachelorhood."

"It can happen to the best of us," Brian joked.

Susan gave him a playful jab in the ribs. "You'd better watch what you say, buster, or you'll get dish detail for the rest of the year."

"On second thought," Brian amended with a soulful expression, "I guess when I was eighteen, I didn't know I'd meet a woman as wonderful as Susan."

"That's better," his wife said dryly.

"I speak only the truth." Brian kissed her forehead, then said to Matt, "Hey, old buddy, come over here and take a gander at our new daughter."

Allison couldn't help noticing the superb fit of Matt's navy pinstripe suit as he walked toward her.

The few moments since his arrival had allowed her to regain her emotional equilibrium, but now his cautious smile and the caress of his dark eyes made her pulses begin to race again. She was relieved when his attention switched to the baby she held.

"Meet Heather O'Shea," Brian said proudly.

"She's awfully little, isn't she?"

"She's five weeks old," said Susan. "If you think she's small now, you should have seen her just after she was born."

"Do you want to hold her?" Allison asked Matt.

"Lord, no. I'd probably drop her or something."

"No, you won't," Allison said, gently unwinding the blanket, then placing the infant into his arms. He looked terrified. Suppressing a grin, she added, "See how easy it is?"

"Relax. You're doing fine," Mr. O'Shea assured him.

"This is a first for me," Matt admitted, carefully shifting his arm so Heather was nestled securely against his chest. "I've never held a baby before."

He looked more confident now, and he was gazing down at Heather with a softness that made Allison's heart twist. Hesitantly he touched the infant's velvety cheek. His brows lifted in surprise as Heather grabbed his finger and refused to let go.

"She's got quite a grip for someone so tiny," he said, laughing. "You must be feeding her Wheaties."

"Hardly," Susan replied. "Babies just naturally hang on to anything that they can get their hands on."

"Isn't she terrific?" Brian said enthusiastically. "So, Matt, when are you going to get married and have one yourself?"

Allison's eyes locked on Matt's, but she couldn't read his expression. Unconsciously she folded her arms across her breasts, wondering again if he was considering marriage. A vivid picture sprang to her mind . . . he was holding his own child, a baby mothered by some other woman. The image caused a strange, stabbing ache in her chest.

"A man can't have a baby. His wife has to have it for him," Susan joked to fill the awkward silence.

"Uh, sorry, I didn't mean to—" Brian began simultaneously, running a hand through his dark red hair.

The strained atmosphere abruptly dissipated as Mrs. O'Shea walked into the living room, wiping her hands on her apron.

"Hello, Brian and Susan." She gave them both a peck on the cheek. "Hello, Matt. It's nice to see you again."

"I'd offer to shake your hand, but I seem to be otherwise occupied at the moment," Matt said, grinning. "I can't figure out how to get Heather to let loose of my finger."

"Here, I'll rescue you," Mrs. O'Shea said, smiling down at her granddaughter. "Come to Grandma, darling." Deftly she unpeeled the tiny fist and took the infant from him.

"I like your apron," said Matt, looking at the smock that covered Mrs. O'Shea's blue dress.

Mrs. O'Shea laughed. "Isn't it nice? It's my favorite."

She held Heather to one side so that everyone could see the bodice of the apron. On it was a picture of Kit in front of a stove, about to put a forkful of spaghetti in her mouth. Kit looked disgruntled as the parrot Kaboodle, who was perched on her shoulder, whispered in her ear, "Taste makes waist."

"Mom's my biggest fan," Allison explained.

"Yeah, all those years I slaved in medical school," Brian complained, "and my sister earns five times what I do by doodling all day long."

"I beg your pardon," Allison said, taking mock offense. "There's a lot more to what I do than that."

"Oh, yeah, how could I forget?" he joked back. "You've also got to color in your drawings for the Sunday comics."

"Brian, stop teasing your sister," Susan chided.

"I'm sorry," he relented, giving Allison a friendly hug. "Seriously, I know how hard you work. You deserve every penny in that big bank account of yours."

"We're all proud of her," said Mr. O'Shea.

Allison was a little embarrassed by the attention. She could sense Matt's gaze burning into her, though she couldn't bring herself to look at him.

Her mother came to the rescue. "Why is everyone standing when there're plenty of places to sit? Please, make yourselves at home." She handed the baby back to Susan. "As for myself, I'd better get back to the kitchen, or we'll never eat."

"And I need to check Heather's diaper," said Susan, trailing her mother-in-law out of the living room.

"Say, how about a quick game of basketball before dinner?" Brian asked Matt.

"Sounds like fun," Matt replied. "Still got the old hoop over the garage door?"

"Sure do. How about you, Dad?"

"Count me in," said Mr. O'Shea. "We'll get Kevin, too."

Allison caught Matt before he could follow her father and brother out the door. "You aren't really serious about playing basketball in this weather, are you?"

"Why not?" he said with a shrug. "The driveway's been shoveled."

"But you're not dressed for it," she argued. "And there's probably ice. You could slip and fall."

"Don't worry, sweetheart. I'll be fine. Now quit fussing, or you'll have me thinking you really care about me."

He bent and kissed her, and the tantalizing brush of his tongue was so brief Allison thought she might have imagined it. At a loss for words, she watched him stride out of the room. He was long gone by the time she thought of a suitable retort. *It's not you I'm worried about; it's my father and brothers.*

But was that really true? She touched her lips, where the taste and feel of his mouth still lingered. Why was it that Matt could reawaken the sensuality in her when other men had tried and failed?

With a sigh of frustration, she headed into the kitchen to help her mother. An hour later, the food was on the table, and everyone was squeezed into the small dining room. Allison was wedged between her brother Kevin and Mrs. O'Shea, with Susan and Brian on the other side of Kevin. Across the table were Colleen, Joe, the twins, and Matt. Mr. O'Shea sat at one end of the table and Allison's grandfather at the other, next to Matt.

Allison was quiet in the boisterous group, listening to the ebb and flow of conversation. Over and over her eyes drifted to Matt. He looked relaxed, his black hair windblown, his skin still glowing from the outdoors. She envied her grandfather, to whom Matt was speaking; answered her mother with uncharacteristic impatience when Mrs. O'Shea unwittingly distracted her; then was angry with herself for letting Matt absorb her attention. Why was she so obsessed with a man she couldn't trust? Hadn't she learned her lesson?

She envisioned a scene where she pretended to seduce him, only to spurn him when he wanted her desperately. No matter how he begged, she wouldn't relent. But the daydream left a bitter taste in her mouth. Deep down she knew she had lost her desire for revenge.

Matt fit in well with their close family group, and she wondered for the first time if he'd been happy growing up an only child. She could picture Thanksgiving dinner with his mother in Boston . . . the stiff white linen set with fine porcelain and polished sterling, the butler hovering in the background.

Allison smiled. That setting was the complete opposite of this one, where everyone was crammed in like sardines, happily eating from several mismatched sets of chipped china. There had been a time, at the age of seventeen, when she had envied Matt his pampered upbringing. Yet now she wouldn't trade this friendly, bantering family of hers for all the money or social status in the world.

After everyone was stuffed to the gills, the women cleared the remains of the feast.

"Why is it that the men always vanish when it's time to do the dishes?" Susan asked dryly as she poured leftover gravy into a plastic container.

"Because they're smart," Mrs. O'Shea replied, smiling.

"And you're going to join them," said Colleen. "You slaved all afternoon fixing this meal. And you run along too, Susan. I'm sure you're tired, with Heather keeping you up nights."

"But you spent all day working at the restaurant," her mother protested.

"True, but this kitchen's too small for all four of us," Allison said firmly.

Colleen shooed them out, then collapsed onto a barstool. "Why do I have a feeling I'm going to regret being so nice?" she groaned, glaring at the mound of dishes piled in the sink. She eased off her high heels, then wiggled her toes with a blissful sigh. "Ah, my feet are killing me!"

"Why don't you pull your stool over to the sink," Allison suggested. "You can rinse, and I'll load the dishwasher."

Her sister positioned herself in front of the sink and turned on the faucet. "I'm glad Thanksgiving only comes once a year," she said, morosely eyeing the protruding belly of her green dress. "In one fell swoop, I've probably put back on the three pounds I lost this week."

"So you did go on a diet, then."

"Well, I decided that nobody was going to lose the weight for me. It's part of my resolution to take charge of my life. I've even been thinking about taking a few college courses on the nights I don't work."

"What in?"

"Oh, general business," Colleen said, scouring a dirty pan. "I don't want to work for someone else forever, so I figured I could get some background in accounting and stuff, then someday open my own restaurant."

"That's a great idea! Have you told Joe yet?"

"Yes." Her sister sighed. "But somehow I don't think he really believes I'm serious."

"Typical male chauvinist," Allison muttered in disgust as she loaded a plate into the dishwasher.

"Now don't blame him," Colleen defended her husband. "He's used to my being dependent on him. He just needs a little time to get accustomed to the new me."

"Maybe so," Allison conceded reluctantly. "Other than that, how are things between you two?"

"We're still not living together, but we're at least communicating—more than we have in years."

They fell silent, each absorbed in their own thoughts as they cleaned up the dishes. It was good that Colleen was finally finding some direction in her life, Allison mused. Now why couldn't she get her own affairs back in order? Lately she'd had the out-of-control feeling of being on a roller coaster. She was rushing downward at meteoric speed . . . and yet there was also a feeling of exhilaration despite the danger of the ride. She longed desperately for things to return to normal.

"So are you going to kill me for inviting Matt here today?"

"What?" Allison jumped at the sound of her sister's voice, nearly dropping the plate she held. "Oh, that," she said, attempting a casual shrug as she closed the dishwasher. "I didn't care one way or the other."

"You two seem to be getting along okay."

"What did you expect? A knock-down, drag-out fight? I can manage to behave like an adult around him."

"Maybe it's none of my business, but do you still love him, even just a little?"

"No, I—"

"Be honest now."

"I *am* being honest. I don't love him."

"Then what do you feel for him?"

Allison bit her lip, glancing over at the kitchen door. It was closed. No one could hear their conversation. She sighed deeply, and plopped down on a barstool opposite her sister.

"I guess I'm not sure anymore—except that I don't despise him, at least not the way I used to."

Shoulders slumped, she stared at the floor. There, she had finally admitted it. But she knew it wasn't just the confession that bothered her; it was the question that followed in its wake. What would fill the void in her emotions now that her hatred had vanished?

"Confused, huh?" Colleen said softly.

Allison looked up and nodded, grateful for her sister's understanding. "I just don't seem to know my own feelings anymore. It's strange . . . I want to be with Matt even though he treated me so cruelly. I'm beginning to wonder if I'm a masochist."

"How do you think he feels about you?"

"He's only interested in sex," Allison said bluntly.

"Are you sure? I mean, from the way he was looking at you at dinner, I got the impression he still cares for you."

Allison waved a hand impatiently. "Still cares? He never loved me in the first place."

"I don't believe that," Colleen disagreed. "I think he wants to patch things up with you. Don't you think it's worth taking the risk—"

"Now wait a minute. Don't get any wild ideas about Matt and me marrying, because it'll never happen."

Colleen smiled, swinging her nylon-stockinged feet. "Alli, you're overreacting. I just wondered where you saw your relationship with him going. He seems awfully interested in you, and since you say you're physically attracted to him, too . . ."

Allison stared at her sister. "Are you suggesting I should have an affair with him?"

"Sure, why not?"

The idea was tempting. It had been at the back of Allison's mind ever since she'd found out that Matt hadn't wanted to take her to bed just so she'd sign that licensing offer. Yet could she cold-bloodedly plan to have an affair with him? She smiled wryly. No, *hot*-bloodedly would be a more accurate description.

"What about all the morals Mom and Dad instilled in us?" she asked.

Colleen shrugged. "Since when does one discreet relationship make a person immoral? It's not as if you sleep with every guy in town." She paused, her expression concerned. "But Alli, are you absolutely certain you're over him? If not, you could really be hurt if things didn't work out."

"Of course I'm over him."

Her attraction to Matt was purely physical, Allison assured herself as they finished the dishes. Yet she was torn between satisfying her desires and protecting her independence. For so many years she had been content with her life. Should she risk losing all that by having an affair with a man she knew she couldn't trust?

She still hadn't made up her mind when she joined everyone in the living room. Restlessly, she flipped through a magazine, half-wishing that Matt would come and talk to her, but he spent most of the evening deep in conversation with Joe.

Finally it was time to leave. She was standing in the hall, sliding her arms into her coat sleeves when she felt big, clearly male hands encircle her waist, turning her around.

"Oh . . . hi," she stammered, looking up at Matt.

He grinned. "Don't sound so thrilled."

His nearness heightened her perceptions. She could smell the subtle tang of his after-shave, hear the throbbing of her blood in her ears, feel the heat of his body. With sudden, sharp longing, she wanted his hands to move upward and touch her breasts. Only pride kept her from melting against him.

"Are you leaving too?" Allison managed.

"I thought I'd follow you home."

Her heart skipped a beat. "Why?"

"Because it's not safe for you to go into an empty house. Any maniac could be waiting there for you." He reached into the closet, found his coat, and put it on.

"Matt, I've been living alone for years. Nothing's ever happened to me."

"I wasn't around then, so I couldn't do anything about it. Now I can."

"But it really isn't necessary—"

"Don't argue," he said crisply, steering her toward the front door. "I'm going to follow you home no matter what you say, so you may as well save your breath."

An independent woman didn't need a man to take care of her, Allison told herself as she zipped along the dark, deserted country road that led to her house. Yet, when she searched her emotions for a justifiable sense of irritation, she failed to find it. Matt's protective attitude only gave her a peculiar sensation of warmth inside.

The headlights of his truck lit the interior of her BMW as he pulled up behind her in the drive. Both of their doors slammed in unison, and Matt joined her at the sidewalk. His fingers spread over the small of her back. Even through the thickness of her coat, the light touch had a faintly possessive feel that awakened all of her nerves.

Inside the house, Winston ambled over, sleepy-eyed, his tail wagging. Matt gave him an absent-minded pat, then glanced in the living room and the library. Allison hung up her coat as he checked the kitchen. She was waiting by the banister when he came down from searching the upstairs bedrooms.

"See? I told you so," she said, unable to keep from smiling.

"Don't get cocky. I only wanted to be sure you were safe."

"There's nothing to worry about. My animals are like a built-in alarm system."

"What, Winston?" Matt scoffed. "If he bothers to get up at all, he'll only lick the burglar's hand."

Winston barked and wagged his tail.

Allison laughed. "Actually, I meant Esmerelda." She drew Matt into the library, where the black cat was curled up in a chair. The animal lifted her head and stared at them, then settled back down to nap.

"If a stranger were in the house, Esmerelda would be upstairs hiding under the bed," she explained. "So, if I come home and she's sleeping here, I know that I'm safe. It's simple but foolproof."

"Somehow I'd feel better if you had an electronic alarm system," Matt said dryly. "Speaking of cats, though, I noticed that the kittens seem to be thriving."

"Yes, Louisa's finally resigned herself to living in the kitchen."

The breath caught in Allison's throat as his eyes flitted to her lips. But he made no move to touch her; instead his hands were jammed into his coat pockets. She was sure her accelerating heartbeat must be audible in the quiet room. Did she want to have an affair with him or didn't she? Confused, she blurted the first thing that came to her mind.

"Thanks for—"

"Would you—" Matt began at the same time.

They looked at each other and laughed.

"Ladies first," he said.

"I, uh, just wanted to thank you for following me home. It wasn't really necessary, but I appreciate the thought."

"Well, I'm glad your family didn't object to my spending Thanksgiving with them. To be truthful, I was a little worried that they still hated me."

"Oh, no," she found herself assuring him. "They enjoyed seeing you again."

"Allison." He paused, and she thought she saw a strange flicker of vulnerability on his face. "I also wanted to ask you if you'd have dinner with me tomorrow night."

"All right."

For an instant, Matt looked taken aback at her easy acceptance. "I'll pick you up at seven, then."

He took a step closer and raised a hand as if to touch her. But before making contact, he abruptly pivoted to move past her and into the hall.

For a split second Allison stared at the empty doorway. Then she was racing out of the library after him, her high heels tapping on the bare pine floor. She caught up to him, putting a hand on his arm just as he was about to open the front door.

"Matt, wait, I—"

I wondered if you'd like to spend the night. She swallowed the reckless words. This was the man who had once taken her love and then dumped her with ruthless disregard. Would she now beg him to stay simply because her body quivered for his touch? Where was her pride?

"I . . . I just wondered what you and Joe were talking about after dinner . . . over at my parents' house," she stammered.

"His construction company put in a bid to do the interior renovating of the mill. We were discussing what needed to be done."

"Oh."

Their eyes locked. Allison was aware of the smooth texture of his overcoat beneath her fingertips, the ruggedness of his features, his subtle masculine scent. The memory of his kiss was so intense she could almost taste it.

"I've got to go." Matt made a sudden move toward the door.

"Without even kissing me good night?"

He stopped, his hand arrested on the doorknob. His jaw muscles flexed as if he were fighting some inner battle. Then slowly he lifted a finger to trace the curve of her lip with the light brush of a moth's wing.

On impulse, Allison slid her arms around his neck and touched her mouth to his. Only a heartbeat's time passed before he responded, gathering her close. His hands combed into the glossy cinnamon silk of her hair in a way that was gentle and cherishing. It was not at all the impassioned embrace she had expected, yet his tenderness stirred her blood more than she would have dreamed possible. It struck her, then, just how lonely she was. She couldn't abide the thought of his leaving. She wanted him to stay with her all night.

Allison pressed herself to him in wanton invitation. Her action unleashed his passion, and his lips became greedy, his tongue demanding. His hands traveled down her spine to the yielding flesh of her derriere, his urgent fingers lifting her to him. Then all at once he let her go so abruptly that she stumbled backward a step.

Opening dazed eyes, Allison saw a flash of raw torment on Matt's face. His sudden restraint bewildered her. Why had he stopped? What was wrong? Didn't he want her?

"Sweet dreams," he murmured.

He was gone before she could form the words to stop him. She leaned her hot forehead against the cool wall, her body still charged with desire. Gradually her physical tumult abated, though an emotional distress lingered. Tears stung her eyes. Gritting her teeth, she refused to let them fall. She hadn't cried in years, and she wasn't going to start now.

Slowly Allison got her turbulent feelings under control and climbed the stairs to her bedroom. The country-furnished room seemed cold and empty tonight. Shivering, she readied herself for bed. But when she crawled between the icy sheets, sleep eluded her.

She stared up at the shadowed ceiling, a humorless smile on her lips as she remembered Matt's parting words. *Sweet dreams.* He suggested the impossible. When it came to Matthew Wakefield, she could only be haunted by bittersweet dreams.

Chapter Seven

*A*llison sat before the oval, wood-trimmed mirror in her bedroom, brushing her hair. Twenty-five strokes, twenty-six. It was amazing how much her life had changed in one week, she mused. Just last Friday, seven brief days ago, Matt had walked back into her life. At the time, she had sworn never to have anything to do with him. But tonight she was about to break that vow. She was going to have an affair with him.

Fifty-two, fifty-three. The brush crackled through her hair, sending silky cinnamon strands floating around her face. Making that choice had lifted a weight from her soul. It wasn't as if she would be manipulating him, she rationalized. He wanted to sleep with her too, so that made things equal. They would be using each other. And besides, why should she continue to fight her physical attraction to him? Having a discreet affair was the best, most logical way to get him out of her system once and for all.

Ninety-one, ninety-two. It had taken most of the day to arrive at her decision. Now that she had made up her mind, nothing, not even the curious foreboding of danger that lurked at the back of her consciousness, could shake that resolve.

One hundred. Allison put the brush down on the dressing table. She twisted the rich, red-brown mass of hair atop her head, fastening it in place. A few wisps escaped to feather her nape. The style made her bare throat look very slender and vulnerable.

On impulse she reached into her jewelry box and found a large diamond hanging from a dainty gold chain. She fastened it around her neck, then fingered the gem for a moment, remembering the day she had gotten it. A lump lodged in her throat, and she had to swallow hard to get rid of it.

She pushed back her stool and stood up. Swiveling, she studied herself in the mirror from all sides. The dress was one she'd bought last year, when she'd paid a visit to the syndication company in New York, attending an obligatory cocktail party. The alluring creation of black silk emphasized her shapely figure. It had a low neckline and an even lower back, dictating that she wear no bra. Only the thinnest of spaghetti straps broke the creamy contour of her shoulders.

For practicality she seldom wore anything but slacks and sweaters, yet her closet held its share of more feminine garments. She loved the feel of satins and silks against her skin. Her lingerie was made from the prettiest, sheerest laces. Her nightgowns were suggestive and clinging, even though she slept alone.

Allison pictured Matt's reaction to her slinky dress, and smiled at her reflection. Tonight she wanted to look sexy and seductive, captivating and coquettish. Because tonight would be a night of romance, stardust, and lovemaking . . . a night to remember.

She stifled the uneasiness that chipped at her confidence. She was after an affair, nothing more. There was no reason to get involved emotionally. She set her shoulders determinedly. It helped to remember that all Matt was looking for was an affair, as well.

Her silk dress whispered as she walked across the bedroom to pick up a tiny black evening bag and her cobwebby shawl shot with gold threads. The doorbell rang as she was heading downstairs. Her blood pulsed with anticipation as she went to open the door.

Beneath his unbuttoned topcoat, Matt wore a navy suit. He held out a bouquet of orchids, and she took it, touched by his thoughtfulness. The blooms ranged from the purest white to the deepest purple, some no larger than her thumbnail, others big and showy. They were all the more exotic considering the barren winter landscape outside.

"For me?" she breathed.

"Actually I brought them for Esmerelda," he teased. "I'm sure she'll appreciate it if you'll put them in water for her."

Allison laid her purse and shawl on the hall table and, still holding the bouquet, she stood on tiptoe and kissed him. He must have shaved before coming

over, because his cheek was smooth beneath her
fingertips and smelled faintly of cologne.

"Thank you," she murmured against his lips.
"From both Esmerelda and me."

His eyes seemed darker than they'd been a moment before. But he made no move to deepen the
kiss or even put his arms around her. A little
disappointed, Allison stepped away to find a vase for
the orchids. Quickly she arranged the flowers and
left them on the captain's table in the library. Then
she slipped into the downstairs powder room
and tucked a mauve bloom into the side of her
chignon.

A silver fox jacket kept her warm as they walked
outside. She carried the shawl over her arm in case
the restaurant was chilly. Stars pricked a purple-
black sky. She took in a deep breath of icy night air,
savoring the clean, refreshing scent. It was an evening made for magic.

"Sorry about the truck," Matt said as they headed
toward town in the Bronco. "I usually drive the
Ferrari on dates."

"Then the Ferrari must get driven a lot."

"Not as often as you think."

Allison didn't reply. She could sense him glance at
her across the darkened interior, but she didn't look
at him. She was too busy trying to convince herself
that it was ridiculous to feel jealous of the other
women in his life. He was hers tonight, and that was
all that mattered. Neither of them owned the other.

They went to a restaurant in town called The
Gardens, which was where her sister worked. The
profusion of potted plants that gave the place its
name were positioned to create a discreet, intimate

atmosphere. Entering the dim foyer, Allison saw Colleen peering down at a reservations list on the podium before her. Her sister looked up and smiled, then came forward to greet them.

"Hi, you guys," she said in a restrained tone befitting her position as hostess. Then, to Matt, "I've saved you our best table, just like you asked."

He grinned. "And to think you did it without a bribe."

"Don't worry, I'll let you know when you can do me a favor sometime," Colleen said with a wink.

They checked their coats. Then Colleen led them over to a booth in a secluded corner of the restaurant. The plush leather seat was in the shape of a semicircle. Its design forced Allison to sit beside Matt, which suited her plans just fine. The linen tablecloth was set with gleaming silver, and the flickering light of a scented candle added to the feeling of intimacy. Colleen handed them menus, and then discreetly withdrew. A few moments later, a waitress brought the fruity white wine Matt had ordered.

"How about a toast?" He raised his glass. "To the loveliest cartoonist I know."

"Some compliment," Allison teased, adjusting the airy gold shawl around her shoulders. "I'm probably the *only* cartoonist you know."

"So you are," he admitted. "And now that I've finally got you all to myself, I can get answers to some questions that have been on my mind."

"Ask away."

"Where do you come up with the ideas for your cartoons?"

Taking a sip of wine, Allison looked at him in

surprise. She'd thought for sure he was going to insist that they discuss their relationship. Of course, he'd find out soon enough that he didn't need to pressure her into having an affair with him.

"Ideas are everywhere. Friends, family, my pets, even magazine articles—you name it, anything can give me an inspiration." She smiled, thinking of the batch of cartoons, based on Louisa's kittens, which she had mailed to the syndication company that morning. "The strips I did this week will be in the newspapers a couple of months from now. Watch for them, and you'll see what I mean."

"Can't you at least give me a hint?" His pleading half-grin made him look boyish despite the mature male angles of his face.

"That depends on what you'll do for me in return," she murmured with a suggestive smile.

Allison lightly ran her fingers over his maroon-and-navy tie, then up over the hard length of his jaw. She was startled when Matt leaned back in his seat, away from her caress. Her hand hovered in midair for a moment before dropping to her lap.

"I guess I'll just have to wait, then," he said smoothly. "So whatever made you want to become a cartoonist?"

Puzzling over his subtle rejection, Allison forced herself to shift mental gears. "Well, you know I've always been interested in art. After I finished college, I moved to New York and got a job with an ad agency. I worked a lot of long hours because I wanted to be a success."

She stared into the clear liquid of her wine. "I was spending so much time at the office and then bringing work home at night so often that I almost forgot how to relax and enjoy myself. That's one of my main objectives in cartooning—to get people to see the humor in their everyday lives even when they're caught up in the rat race. I want to make them laugh because they identify with the funny things that happen to Kit and Kaboodle. I guess the comic strip is sort of a reflection of the way I view life."

She looked at Matt, unsure of why she was confiding to him things she'd never told anyone else. His expression was hard to read in the dim light of the booth. "Are you sure you're interested in all this?"

"Of course. Please, go on."

"Anyway, I lived alone in New York, and it seemed like my job was my whole life—so I drew some cartoons that made a joke out of how career-oriented I had become. You know, like a picture of me at my desk surrounded by piles and piles of papers, thinking: 'One of these days I'm going to get to the bottom of all this. I only hope there're still a few eligible men left when I'm sixty-five years old.'"

Matt frowned. "I don't understand. Surely you had a lot of dates."

"Actually, no," Allison admitted. "I spent most of my time working."

"I find that hard to believe."

"Why?"

"That's obvious, isn't it? You're a sensual, passionate woman, not to mention lovely, intelligent, desirable . . ."

He leaned forward, into the soft circle of light cast by the candle, and lifted a gentle hand to her nape. The breath caught in her throat at the desire burning in his dark eyes. She felt the gauzy gold shawl slip from her shoulders. It was unnerving, she thought dazedly, how much she was in his power when he looked at her like that. He could do whatever he pleased, demand whatever he wanted, and she would be incapable of resistance.

His fingers traced the line of her jaw, then skimmed down her throat to the narrow strap over one bare shoulder. As if in a trance, he watched the movement of his hand. Knowing that he wanted her enhanced the sensual pleasure she felt. Her nipples strained against the thin black silk of her bodice. In a moment he would pull her roughly to him and kiss her. . . .

Abruptly, a remote look shadowed his eyes and he dropped his hand. "Allison, we need to—"

The arrival of the waitress with their entrées cut short whatever Matt had been about to say. When she was gone, he guided the conversation onto neutral topics such as Allison's family and his plans for renovating the textile mill.

Allison toyed with her food, debating whether or not to ask him to complete his sentence. We need to—what? Talk? Stop seeing each other?

She didn't understand why he had suddenly pulled back into himself like that. Was he being cautious because of the way they'd argued the past few times they'd seen each other? It was the only explanation she could think of to account for his strange behavior. And if that were true, then she'd have to drop a blatant hint to convince him that now she did want him.

With a seductive smile, Allison used her fork to spear a bite of shrimp from her plate.

"This is heavenly. Would you like a taste?"

Without waiting for a reply, she popped the succulent morsel into his mouth. Then she slid her fork under another piece, eating it herself. She saw his eyes follow the tip of her tongue as she licked a trace of spicy sauce from her lips.

"Did you like that?" she asked throatily.

"Delicious." The word sounded forced.

"How about another bite?"

"Please . . . don't." His hand came down over her wrist as she was lifting her fork. She was perplexed by the strain in his voice. "I'll never be able to finish my own dinner if I eat yours," he explained in a more normal tone. "Now, you never got through telling me about what it feels like to be a star." He released her wrist to eat his steak.

Allison took a sip of wine, miffed by his smooth rejection. His behavior was frustrating. He *did* want her; she could see it in his eyes. So why was he acting so cool?

"I'd hardly call myself a star," she replied.

"You are to your readers. Do you get many fan letters?"

She lifted a shoulder. "Oh, some."

"Do you ever answer them?"

"I try to. I figure if a person feels strongly enough about the strip to write to me, I owe him or her a personal answer."

"Well, success doesn't seem to have spoiled you."

Allison smiled. "Whenever I get to thinking I'm really hot stuff, I go take a very cold shower."

"Is that the only reason you take cold showers?"

They stared at each other. Again she felt that sexual tension in the air between them, as tangible as the glass of wine in her fingers. It was heating her blood and accelerating her pulse. She couldn't understand him. First he retreated, then he advanced. She was beginning to think he was trying to drive her insane.

"Sorry. I had no right to say that," Matt said, letting his fork drop with an abrupt clatter. "Mind if I smoke?"

Allison shook her head. She watched in silence, sipping her wine as he fished a pack of cigarettes and a gold lighter out of his pocket.

"Care for dessert?" he asked.

"I will if you will," she answered. "They make the most scrumptious chocolate pistachio torte here—"

"Well, hello. Aren't you Matt Wakefield?" a syrupy female voice purred. "I heard you were back in town. You've been out of touch so long I almost didn't recognize you."

Allison frowned, looking up at the colt-legged blonde in a shapely ice-blue dress who stood beside the table, smiling at Matt. The woman was a passing acquaintance. Candy had been one of those girls who had tried, and failed, to steal Matt's attention away from her that summer so long ago.

"I'm sorry," he said pleasantly, placing his cigarette in the ashtray to take her outstretched hand. "You look familiar, but I'm not sure I remember—"

"Candy Reeves," Allison supplied. "Or are you going by the name Phillips again?" It was silly, this spurt of jealousy she felt. But did Matt hold the blonde's hand for a moment longer than politeness dictated? Instinct made her move closer to him, laying her fingers on his arm to mark her prior claim.

"Reeves," Candy clarified, ignoring Allison's possessive gesture. "It was my husband's name."

"Tom Reeves?" Matt asked. "Ah, yes, I remember now. You two were on-again, off-again that summer I was lifeguarding at the community center pool."

"Well, it's off permanently, I'm afraid," Candy said with a woeful pout. "Tom just never understood me, so now I'm all by myself again."

"I'm sorry to hear that," he sympathized.

"It's hard to be a divorcée in a quiet little place like Copperwood," the blonde went on with a sigh. "There aren't very many eligible men around. It's nice to know that another handsome bachelor has moved into town."

How much more blatant could you get? Allison wondered in disgust. Candy was an appropriate name for the woman. She was like a bit of cotton candy, all sugar and fluff, with nothing to offer but a moment of sensual enjoyment.

Allison dropped her hand from Matt's arm, trying to ignore the little voice inside her head that whispered: *And that's all Matt's looking for, sensual enjoyment to pass the time while he's in town. He could get what he wants just as easily from another woman . . . a woman like Candy Reeves.*

"Well, I've got to be on my way," Candy told him. "If you ever get lonely, feel free to look me up. I'm in the book."

"If I remember correctly, you always had quite a busy schedule, Candy," he bantered.

"I'm always willing to make time for you. See you around." Candy waltzed away, her hips swaying suggestively.

Matt turned to Allison, stubbing out his cigarette in the ashtray. "Ready for that dessert now?"

"Hmmm? No . . . no, I don't think so. I'd just as soon leave, if you don't mind."

"Why?" He frowned. "I thought we'd stay awhile and talk."

"We can talk back at my house."

"And why not here?"

Allison picked up her shawl and purse, unable to understand the irrational anger inside her that had swept the magic out of the night. The secluded booth no longer seemed intimate. The candlelit setting had become tawdry rather than romantic.

"If you're so anxious to stay here, Matt," she said tightly, "then I'm sure Candy would be more than willing to keep you company. I'm leaving."

He grabbed her bare shoulders as she tried to slide out of the curved seat. "Allison, what the hell is wrong with you? Why are you—" He stopped, staring at her in disbelief. "Surely you're not jealous. . . are you?"

She didn't answer, unable to trust her voice. Mortified, she turned her head aside, biting her lower lip, ashamed of the silly emotional weakness in her that made her chin tremble.

"Allison."

He said her name with a tender half-laugh, pulling her into his arms so that her face was buried in the smooth material of his jacket. His hands were warm on her bare back as he held her in a tight embrace. She felt his breath stir her hair. After a moment, he tilted her jaw with his finger.

"Whatever gave you the wild idea that I was interested in Candy?"

"You were flirting with her," Allison forced out.

"I was making idle conversation," he corrected. "It didn't mean anything."

"But all you want from me is sex," she blurted. "You could get it just as easily from her."

Matt looked away for an instant, the muscles in his jaw tensing. His arm held her trapped against his warm body. He bent and put his lips to the veil of wispy bangs that covered her forehead.

"I think it's about time you and I had a serious talk," he murmured. "Let's go back to your house."

He motioned to their waitress, and paid the check. During the ride home, Allison wondered what he had to say. He wanted to have an affair and so did she, so what was there to discuss?

She was still puzzling over it as she hung up her silver fox jacket at home. They went into the library, where she turned on several lights, bathing the room in a soft glow. Then she kicked off her high heels, digging her toes into the thick Bokhara rug.

"Why don't you make a fire, while I fix us both a drink," she suggested. "What would you like?"

"Scotch, if you have some. On the rocks." Matt was removing his jacket, getting ready to put a log on the grate.

"Coming right up."

Allison headed down the hall, lost in thought. Why had Matt acted so restrained earlier this evening, and why was he now interested only in talking? Entering the kitchen, she stepped over Winston, snoozing on the floor in front of the door. She poured the drinks and took an absentminded sip of her amaretto. Maybe Matt no longer desired her . . .

"Raawwkk!" commented Mr. Screech. The parrot then gave a loud wolf whistle.

"Thanks for the vote of confidence." Allison smiled as she drew a cloth over the brass bird cage. She had to be misreading Matt's actions. He wanted her; she could see it in his eyes when he looked at her. He was probably just being cautious because of their last confrontation. So maybe it was time to take matters into her own hands. If he wouldn't make the first move, then she would have to seduce him. It was as simple as that.

Picking up their glasses, she tiptoed out of the kitchen, careful not to disturb Louisa and the kittens, sleeping peacefully in the box of old clothing. When she reentered the library a fire was snapping in the hearth, casting mysterious shadows in the corners of the room. Matt was standing with one elbow perched on the mantelpiece. He was staring off into the distance, a brooding look on his face. Seeing her, he came forward and took his drink.

"Thanks, I needed this." Taking a swallow of Scotch, he seated himself on one of the smoky-blue love seats that flanked the fireplace. "Sit down," he said, gesturing at the sofa opposite him. "We need to talk."

He closed his eyes and rubbed at the frown on his forehead. Allison smiled, quietly placing her glass of amaretto on the captain's table, alongside the vase of orchids. Then she reached for the back of her dress. The crackle of the fire concealed the soft whisper of the zipper as she slid it down.

Chapter Eight

*I*t might have been her subtle feminine scent or simply an inner radar that made Matt sense Allison's closeness a split second before he felt her small, soft body melt into his lap. He'd been agonizing over the best way to say what was on his mind. How does a man go about telling the woman he'd once rejected so cruelly that he still loves her, that it had all been a mistake, and could she please give him a second chance?

But before he could come to any conclusion, his eyelids snapped open in response to her nearness. There was a rustle of silk as Allison nestled herself onto his thighs. Her soft little smile made his blood begin to pound. His fingers tightened around the glass of Scotch that was resting on the arm of the sofa, his other hand automatically encircling her, coming to rest on the bare skin revealed by her low-backed dress.

"What the hell do you think you're doing?" he demanded, uncertain of which he wanted to do more, kiss her or kill her for distracting him.

"You told me to sit down." She widened innocent green eyes and wound her arms around his neck.

"You know I meant across from me, not on top of me."

"But I prefer being close to you," she purred. "I should think you'd be flattered."

"I am," he growled in a tight voice that implied he was anything but. "Now will you kindly pick up your darling little behind and get over to where you belong?"

"This is where I belong."

Allison put her mouth to his neck. He sucked in his breath, feeling the moist, arousing path of her tongue over his flesh. Her fragrance was all woman. Now she was nibbling along his jaw. He knew he should stop her, but he couldn't summon the will-power. Ignoring the dictates of his brain, his hand slid up her spine to the back of her head, gently surrounding the coil of hair. His fingers brushed the delicate petals of the orchid that was tucked into her chignon. The flower felt as soft as her skin.

God, he should have known it was a mistake to leave the relative safety of the restaurant, where succumbing to temptation had its limits. She'd made it clear all throughout dinner that, for whatever reasons, she had decided she was willing to have an affair. But he wanted more than a few stolen mo-ments of physical ecstasy. If their relationship was ever going to have half a chance, they had to first get to know each other again. That was the way it had to be. That was the way it *must* be. Gritting his teeth, Matt dropped his hand to her bare shoulder and pushed her back.

"Stop it, Allison. That's enough."

"Don't be such a grouch," she responded, reaching for his tie. "Here, let me loosen this for you. That'll make you feel better."

"We need to talk," he said firmly.

"Later. Now we've got more important things to do."

She unknotted his tie and tossed it aside, unbuttoning the collar of his shirt. Lips parted seductively, she cupped his face in her hands.

"Allison, I mean it—" he began with a hint of desperation. His blood was racing at the sultry look in her green eyes.

He was silenced by the silky touch of her tongue on his lips. Matt kept his teeth rigidly clenched in determined resistance. If it killed him, he wouldn't forget how necessary it was to avoid getting involved physically at this critical point in their relationship.

Undaunted, she nibbled at his mouth, the tip of her tongue enticing his flesh. She was leaning into his chest, and through their clothing he could feel the beguiling softness of her breasts. Her fingers lightly caressed the hair at his temples. The gentle pressure of her thigh tantalized his aroused sex.

Concentrate, he ordered himself. *Think about the crackling sound of the fire, the icy smooth glass in your hand, anything to keep from responding.*

But everything she did made his willpower crumble a little more. With a muffled groan, he finally succumbed to temptation, opening his mouth to let her taste him intimately. One kiss, he swore silently, that was all he'd allow himself.

His tongue played with hers, his free hand cupping her hair as he drank deeply of her sweetness. His other arm came around her, fingers still clutching the glass, the faint clinking sound of the ice cubes lost to the lure of his other senses. For one long, steamy moment, he let himself revel in the heady feeling of holding and kissing and caressing the woman he loved. It was with the utmost reluctance that he finally dragged his lips free, resting his chin on the crown of her head while he tried to get his respiration rate under control.

"You taste like almonds," he murmured.

He couldn't see her face because it was tucked into his neck, but he felt her smile.

"It's the amaretto I was drinking," she said huskily, touching his skin with her tongue.

"Stop that." Matt seized her shoulder and pushed her upright. "The fun's over, and now we're going to talk."

"Why? Don't you want to make love to me?" Playfully, Allison began unbuttoning his shirt.

"Believe me, there's nothing I'd like more, but . . ." There was a pause, then he exclaimed, "What the hell . . . !"

He had slid his hand down her spine, only to realize when his fingers encountered a smooth expanse of bare skin all the way to her waist that her zipper was undone.

"Oh, gosh, I almost forgot . . . I wanted to make

things easier for you," she said, lips tilted into a grin that was half-sexy, half-impish. "Hey, don't you dare do that!"

She squirmed and twisted as he tried to refasten her dress. The glass he held hampered him and, before he could stop her, she let the spaghetti straps slip off her shoulders, the black silk pooling at her waist.

Jaw tensing, Matt stared at her beautiful naked breasts. He'd suspected from the moment he'd picked her up this evening that she wasn't wearing a bra. The cut of her bodice had told him that, and the knowlege had tortured him throughout dinner.

"Feel how fast my heart is beating for you," Allison murmured, taking his unresisting hand and pressing it against the warm skin just above the soft sweet curve of her breast.

He felt the quick flutter of her heart beneath his palm. As if in a trance, he watched his hand begin a slow descent until he was cradling the tender swell of her breast. His thumb made an arc across the hardened tip. Allison's eyelids drifted shut, her head tilting back to expose the slender white expanse of her throat. The room was silent except for the hiss of the fire and the faint, sighing, wildly arousing sounds emerging from her parted lips.

God help him, he wanted nothing more than to take each honey-gold nipple into his mouth. In the long lonely years he and Allison had been apart, he'd had plenty of other women. But they'd bored him after one or two dates. There had been no emotional entanglements because no woman had ever claimed his heart, his soul, his mind the way

Allison had. Never had he ever hovered on the brink of losing complete control over his power of reasoning, as he did now, by the mere sight and touch of a naked breast.

Reason warred with primitive instinct. He knew that if he wanted to keep from ruining any chance of building a meaningful relationship with Allison again, he had to put a halt to his burgeoning passion. Right now. Lips tight, pulse beating hot and hard, Matt dragged his hand away, coiling his fingers into a tight fist to erase the feel of her breast from his palm.

"Get up, Allison. The fun's over."

It was a crisp lash of a voice, like the one he used in the boardroom to issue orders. Her eyes fluttered open, and she focused on him, tilting her head in bewilderment.

"What?"

"I said, *get up!*"

"There's no need to shout."

There was a tiny tremor of hurt in her tone as she scrambled off his lap. As she backed away, the unzipped dress slithered down over her hips, the silk whispering over her nylons as it fell into a heap on the rug. She made no move to stop its descent. Unsmiling, watching him steadily, she peeled off her lacy black half-slip. Her shapely body was silhouetted by the fire in the hearth behind her.

Stunned, Matt was slow to react. It was only when she put her hands to the waistband of her pantyhose that he surged to his feet.

"Dammit, Allison, put your clothes back on this instant!"

An anger born of a desperate attempt to hold onto

his self-control made him snap at her. Her eyes widened, and her hands paused in midmotion before crossing protectively over her naked breasts.

"You really don't want me, do you?"

Her stricken expression was an echo of the way she had looked the day he'd had to tell her he was ending their relationship. That sight had nearly destroyed him then. The knowledge that he had hurt her again made his chest tighten. He fought a strong impulse to go to her. It was only when he realized that the glistening sheen in her eyes was tears that he knew he had lost.

"Oh, Christ," he muttered.

He took a step toward her, then remembered the drink that was still clutched in his hand. He drained it in one burning gulp, slamming the empty glass onto the captain's table. Closing the distance between them with one stride, he folded her in his strong embrace.

"Allison, Allison," he murmured, "you couldn't be more mistaken. I do want you . . . I'm aching for you."

"Then why did you reject me? What's wrong with me?" Her voice was broken and muffled against his shoulder. "What a fool you must think I am!"

"That's not true." He tipped her chin up, and his heart twisted as he saw her big green eyes glossed with tears. "Allison, honey, how could I not want you? You're so lovely, so desirable . . . I can't begin to tell you what you do to me inside."

"Then show me," she begged, sliding her hands inside the gaping front of his shirt. "Please, Matt, I need you."

He stared down at her, wrestling with the remnants of rationality. She felt small and defenseless in his arms, yet she had him completely in her power. Unknowingly she had switched to a far more dangerous seduction technique. How could he refuse her when she was appealing to his heart as well as his soul?

"Allison, I—" He hesitated, clinging to a last lingering bit of restraint. "Oh, hell!"

With an odd, despairing laugh, he tightened their embrace. Then he was kissing her again, this time with a fierce but tender passion that destroyed once and for all his chances of resisting the lure of her body.

His hands glided along her spine, drinking in the satiny texture of her skin. His fingers curled into her soft behind and molded her to the hot ache in his loins. He lifted his head and gazed down at her. He thought he would drown in the iridescent green of her eyes.

With mounting eagerness, they undressed each other. Matt tore off his silver cuff links and tossed them with a clatter onto the captain's table. Allison then helped him remove his shirt. Discarding the rest of his clothing, he knelt before her. With trembling hands, he peeled away her nylons and lacy black panties until the only thing adorning her naked body was the diamond pendant around her neck.

Gripping her waist, he looked up at her, marveling at her loveliness. Her skin had a golden glow bestowed by the flames on the hearth; her bone structure was fragile and fine. She might have been a goddess, or a perfectly sculpted statue. Yet she was all warm human flesh and blood, and she wanted him.

A surge of powerful emotion left him shaking. His woman. Matt let the illusion envelop him. It never ceased to amaze him, the magic and mystery of his feelings for her. He ached to tell her of his love, but he couldn't, not just yet, not until he had the leisure to explain everything to her first.

He drew Allison to her knees before him. One of her hands rested on the thatch of black curling hair that covered his chest while the other touched his aroused masculinity. His passion flared. With a deep groan, he pulled her down onto the carpet in front of the hearth, the heat of the fire no match for the flames within him.

Her body was small and lithe beneath him. Her throat was arched, and the pins that had fastened her chignon in place had scattered, so that glossy cinnamon strands streamed over the rug like skeins of spun silk.

He ran his fingers through the thick tresses, then paused to look down at her. Firelight gleamed over her body, softening the already gentle feminine slopes and valleys. His fingers meandered over her breasts and flat belly, finally dipping into the dewy warmth between her thighs, stroking her until he felt her tremble. Her faint sighs mingled with the sounds of his own ragged breathing and the crackling of the fire.

"How I've needed you . . ." he whispered, his voice deep and husky.

Matt felt a wave of almost unbearable desire at the passion reflected on her face. Yet he held himself

back, suppressing the urge to satisfy his own hunger
without first giving her pleasure. He put his mouth to
her thigh, and moved upward, relearning every part
of her until he knew her ardor matched his own.
Then he took her with a fierce, flaring need, thrusting deeply into the very core of her, submerging his
body in hers. She wrapped him in the silken web of
her arms and legs, her hips rising to his in a driving,
erotic rhythm.

This was what he wanted! This joyous union with
the woman he loved, a life together forevermore,
this perfect joining of body and soul. He heard her
cry aloud as the release burst upon her, and the wild
exaltation he felt sent him tumbling over the edge
himself, hoarsely calling out her name, his strong
body trembling with ecstasy.

Allison was floating, lost in that special deep
satisfaction she hadn't felt for many years, not since
that long-ago weekend on Martha's Vineyard. It was
a time of delicious lassitude, this aftermath of slow-
ing heartbeats and cooling bodies. The thick rug
cushioned her back. Matt's weight was sprawled
over her, a heavy yet welcome burden. Her face was
tucked into his damp neck, and she breathed in his
male scent.

When he had resisted her attempts to seduce him,
at first she'd thought it was only because he wanted
to control her. After all, he was used to being in
charge. Then, thinking that he didn't want her at all,
she had felt so wretchedly miserable that she'd
wanted to die, just as when he'd told her he didn't
really want to marry her, that he'd only been

overcome by his passion for her. She shuddered at the memory.

"Cold?" Matt lifted his head, shifting his powerful body so that he lay beside her, jaw propped on his hand.

"Oh . . . I must have felt a draft or something. You'll just have to keep me warm." She curled against him, winding her arms around his neck.

"My pleasure." Hugging her close, he smiled down at her with such tenderness that her heart melted. How lovely it was going to be to have an affair with him. His eyes were a deep amber in the firelight. She basked in their glow as he smoothed a few stray strands of hair away from her face. Abruptly his gaze hardened, and she could feel a sudden, coiled tension in his muscles.

"Who gave you this?"

Against her nape, she felt a slight tug of the gold chain. The round diamond was resting in Matt's palm. She stirred uneasily, wondering why she had worn it.

"Does it matter?" she countered.

"To me it does." There was a jealous edge to his voice. "It's the sort of gift a man would give. Are you still seeing him?"

"As a matter of fact, yes."

He flinched, his face growing grimmer. "Are you going to keep on dating him . . . after what we shared tonight?"

"Why not?" she said with a wicked smile. "He and I've got a good thing going."

There was a silence, then Matt ground out, "Who is he?"

He looked a little dangerous, but also a little hurt. His fingers tightened around the diamond as if he contemplated tearing it from her neck. Allison knew she had to tell him.

"You," she said simply.

Matt frowned in obvious bafflement. "But I never gave you a necklace like this."

"It's the diamond from my engagement ring," she explained. "I had it reset and made into a pendant."

"Ah . . . so you did." His expression lightened. "I figured you'd sold that ring to help pay for your college expenses. What made you keep it?"

"I don't know. Impulse, I guess." Allison shrugged with more nonchalance than she felt. Why *had* she kept the ring that held such painful memories? Several years ago she had found it tucked into a corner of her jewelry box. Something, she wasn't sure what, had impelled her to have this necklace fashioned.

"You know, tonight is the anniversary of the first time we made love," Matt said softly. "That was twelve years ago."

"I . . . I had forgotten," she lied.

"Well, I haven't. That's why you and I need to talk."

That again. To avoid his gaze, Allison stared down at his hand, which rested at her waist. His skin was dark against her creamy complexion. How strong his fingers were, she mused, yet how gently they could touch her.

"Allison?" Matt tilted her chin back up. "We have to discuss our relationship sometime. There's no avoiding it."

"I don't understand why it's so important that we talk. We both want to have an affair, so why analyze it to death?"

"But you're wrong," he said. "We both *don't* want to have an affair."

Allison stared at him in astonishment. "How can you say that after what just happened? You wanted me just as much as I wanted you."

"I won't argue that." He sighed heavily. "Look, I didn't come here tonight intending to make love to you. It's just that you're one hell of a persuasive woman."

She rolled away from him and sat up, hugging her knees. Her brain felt like it was made of wood. Matt was saying that for him, tonight had been a mistake. He desired her but he didn't want to have an affair. She tensed, the delicious lazy lassitude of their lovemaking dissipating until her body felt chilled to the bone. Now it was becoming clearer. He was rejecting her, just as he had years ago. And she knew why.

"It isn't necessary for us to have any little talk," she snapped in anger. "I don't need to hear again that I'm too low-class for you! So why don't you just get out of here and out of my life!"

Fury sent adrenaline coursing through her veins. She leaped to her feet, intending to storm out of the room before the hot prickling in her eyes turned to tears. But Matt's hand shot up and snared her wrist before she could take more than a step. In one sinuous movement he was standing in front of her, hauling her against his naked chest. She tried to wriggle free, but his grip was like a steel trap.

"You've got this all wrong! If you'd just listen—"

"Listen?" she blazed back, continuing to struggle. "So you can tell me again that I'm not good enough for you? That my blood isn't blue enough for anything more than a quick roll in the hay? That you'd like me to keep out of your hair after tonight? Well, it isn't necessary; I can take a hint. I don't have any intention of making a fool of myself over you again!"

"If you'd cool down that hot Irish temper of yours, you'd see how illogical you're being," Matt ground out, giving her shoulders a quick shake. "Why would I invite you out to dinner if I was ashamed to be seen with you? Why would I bother going to your parents' house yesterday if I thought they were beneath me? And why the hell would I spend every waking minute trying to dream up excuses to be with you?"

Abruptly she went still. "I don't understand."

"That's precisely why we need to talk."

Allison stared into his eyes, trying to read his expression. Deep inside of her a sense of foreboding stirred, making her feel oddly like a cornered animal. Did she really want to get into a serious discussion with him? Instinct told her there was danger in relating to this man on any plateau other than the physical.

With a muffled thud, a burning log settled in the hearth. She took a deep breath. Surely she was being melodramatic. What could Matt say that could threaten her in any way?

"All right," she agreed finally. "We'll talk."

He released her, and they both pulled on their

clothing. While Matt added another log to the fire, Allison made a desultory attempt to repin her hair, finally abandoning the effort and letting her hair float in riotous disarray to her bare shoulders. Something on the floor, almost camouflaged by the ruby reds of the rug, caught her eye. She bent and picked it up. It was the orchid that had adorned her chignon, ánd miraculously, it was uncrushed.

Matt had left his shirt unbuttoned, revealing the dark hair on his chest. He drew her over to one of the love seats, and they sat down. Still clasping the orchid, Allison settled herself into the circle of his arm, leaning into his hard body, her bare feet tucked beneath the black silk of her skirt.

He looked at her with a hint of humor. "I hope I can trust you not to seduce me again."

"I don't understand why you're so opposed to our making love," she said defensively.

"Because we've been apart for twelve years. We've both changed a lot, and we need time to get to know each other again before we jump into a physical relationship."

"But if we're going to have an affair, all that really matters is that we're compatible in bed." With a provocative smile, she slid a hand inside his shirt to caress his chest. "And there's no doubt that we do get along well in that respect."

Matt heaved a deep sigh. "I can't deny that, but I still think we need to get a few things straightened out. Allison, have you thought about what I told you? About the real reasons I broke our engagement?"

"No, I haven't," she said flatly, letting her hand

drop to her lap. "Frankly, Matt, your story was a little hard to swallow. If you'd really loved me, you wouldn't have given up so easily."

"But at the time I honestly thought I was doing what was best for you. I knew how much you wanted to go to art school, and how could I ask you to give that up?"

"I never asked for a life of luxury."

"I didn't think you'd have wanted poverty, either," he argued. "There was no way I could have supported a wife, and my parents were having a tough enough time with the business. They couldn't have afforded the expense of college for the both of us. We both would have had to go to work, and I just couldn't let you do that."

Allison gave a cynical laugh. "Are you so sure about that? Your parents never thought I was good enough for their only son and heir. It wouldn't surprise me to learn they blew that story of a crisis at Wakefield Mills way out of proportion just to get you to dump me."

"Is that what you really believe?" Matt stared at her in amazement. "Allison, I was there. I know how bad it was. The company didn't fully recover until maybe five years ago."

She frowned, wondering for the first time if she might have misjudged him. "But how could a company on the verge of bankruptcy make such a remarkable recovery?"

"Because I'm in charge now," he said matter-of-factly. "Much as I loved my father, he wasn't a good businessman. Right around the time you and I broke up, a glut had developed in the textile market, and Wakefield Mills was one of the firms that was worst hit. Unfortunately, my father had authorized the building of two new plants that ended up sitting virtually idle. But the company still had to pay for them, and that's what pushed us almost to the point of bankruptcy."

"And why didn't you know about all this before you asked me to marry you?"

"Because I was only eighteen. My parents didn't want to worry me, so they kept it secret for as long as they could."

"Until they discovered the poor choice you'd made for a wife." Allison couldn't keep the bitterness from her voice.

"That's not the way it happened."

But for a brief instant there was a flash of guilt on his face. It told her she was right. Matt might not admit it, but his parents *had* played a role in the breakup. How different her life would have been if she had measured up to the Wakefields' standards of breeding.

"So tell me how the business was saved," she said, deliberately letting the topic of his parents' opinion of her die.

"My father managed to make some deals with our creditors. There were a few rough years, and I tried to help out as much as I could, even though at the time I didn't know much about running a big corporation."

"Well, of course not. You were only in college."

"No, I wasn't. I quit Harvard and never went back."

She stared, struggling to believe him. "Things were really that bad?"

"In a word, yes." He shrugged. "Leaving school

was all for the best, though. I learned more on the job than I could have from any textbook. I had a crash training course in textiles, including everything from several months at a knitting mill to a few more selling the finished product. It was a couple of years before I was able to offer a knowledgeable opinion in the decision-making. My father was pleased with some of the ideas I came up with, and I guess the board was too, because after he died, I was named chief executive."

"You make it sound so simple."

Matt smiled. "It was a lot of hard work and long hours." His arm tightened around her, and he touched her cheek. "But through it all, Allison, I never forgot you, never stopped missing you."

The warmth in his eyes made her heart twist. Confused, Allison looked down at the orchid she still clutched in her hand. Unconsciously her fingers were crushing the fragile mauve petals. She set the bloom on the cushion beside her, slowly raising her troubled gaze to his.

"Why, Matt?" she whispered. "Why did you have to come back? Why couldn't you have left me alone?"

"I couldn't stay away," he said gently. "For years, I had myself convinced that I didn't deserve anything from you, not after I'd hurt you so badly. But I was lonely. Then one day it hit me that maybe there might still be a remote chance for us. Once I got it into my mind, I couldn't stop thinking about it. So I dreamed up that licensing offer. I figured you'd refuse to sign it, and that would give me an excuse to see you while I was in town."

"But why were you lonely? Surely there are plenty

of women around who would be more than happy—"

"I don't want any other woman," Matt broke in. He picked up her hand and stroked it. "I told you I lied back then about not wanting to marry you. That's the truth, Allison. It was a stupid mistake on my part, but I hope to God it's not too late to undo it."

She shifted uneasily, feeling a prickling of panic. "What exactly are you saying, Matt?"

He hesitated for a long moment. When he finally spoke, his voice was low and husky with emotion. "I want more than just an affair. I still love you, Allison, now more than ever. I want to marry you."

A glob of resin on one of the logs suddenly popped, but Allison scarcely heard it. Her whole being was focused on absorbing Matt's incredible words. She felt as though she was suffocating. He had to be lying!

"You can't possibly mean that," she said shakily.

"Yes, I do, every word."

The intensity of his eyes and tightness of his grip on her hand made it plain that he was dead serious. Matt loved her. He really and truly loved her. She restrained a cowardly urge to bolt out of the room and get as far away as possible. Oh, dear God, why had this happened? She bit her lip, trying to make sense out of the tumult in her brain. One thought shone through with crystal clarity. Anything beyond a physical relationship with him was out of the question.

"Matt, I would have given the world to have heard you say that years ago. But now?" She shook her head emphatically, pulling her hand free. "It could never work. All I want from you is an affair. Nothing more. *Nothing.*"

His expression turned pensive, quiet, sad. "I expected you to react like that. All I'm asking for right now is a little time—time for us to get to know each other again and make sure we're not throwing away a future together."

"Even if I were to consider it—and I'm not saying that I would—it couldn't ever work. I hated you for so many years, Matt. Even if someday I could forgive you, how could I forget my gut-level feelings for you? Or trust you again?"

"Do you still hate me?" he asked softly.

She took a deep, steadying breath, knowing he deserved the truth. "No. No, I can't honestly say that I do."

"And what do you feel for me, then?"

"I don't really know," she admitted, threading a hand into her disheveled hair. "This is all happening so fast."

"Then if your emotions can change in the space of a week, who's to say they might not change again? If you gave it a chance, maybe you *could* love me again."

"That will never happen!" Feeling trapped, Allison shot up from the sofa and marched over to the fireplace, twirling on slender legs to face him. "And what about the other side of the coin? Your emotions could change too, you know. Suppose *you* stop loving *me* once you get to know me again."

"There are no guarantees," he conceded quietly. "You'll just have to take a chance."

"That's out of the question! Look what happened the last time I trusted you. No, all I want is a physical relationship. It's an affair or nothing. Take your pick."

It was a standoff. They glared at each other, Allison with her chin tilted, her hands on her hips, and Matt frowning, his spine rigid against the sofa cushions. She was going to win the battle of the wills, she vowed. After all, she could always seduce him, but there was no way he could force her to fall in love with him.

Then the anger faded from his eyes, and his expression became speculative. He got up and paced the length of the library. His silence was grating on her nerves, and she was about to ask him what he was thinking when he pivoted to face her, hands jammed in his pockets.

"You leave me no other choice," he said decisively. "I'll just have to move in here with you."

She laughed nervously. That was not the sort of discreet relationship she had envisioned. "You must be joking."

"I was never more serious in my whole life."

"You want to live here with me like . . . like *roommates?*" she asked, struggling to sort through the ramifications.

"Live in the same house, share meals, spend our free time together . . . and, of course, sleep in the same bed."

She shook her head. "That's out of the question."

"Think about it for a minute," he urged. "It's the perfect compromise. If we live together, you get your affair and I have my chance to get to know you again."

Allison leaned weakly against the mantel. She was tempted, she admitted to herself. To have the leisure to make love whenever they wanted to . . . The prospect made her pulse leap. But there were too many other considerations.

"Suppose people were to find out?" she asked. "This is a small town, and word does get around. It's not that I'd be ashamed or anything, but I wouldn't want to upset my parents."

"They know you're a big girl," Matt reasoned. "And I can keep my apartment in town as a cover. No one need ever find out about us."

"But there're other things to think about, too. Chores, for one. I'm used to having only myself to pick up after."

"We'll split everything down the middle, fifty-fifty, including cleaning and living expenses."

Allison cocked her head in doubt. "I just don't think I could adjust after living alone for so long. For all I know, you might distract me from my work, upset my routine . . ."

"But you'll never know if it could work if you refuse to give it a try." Matt approached her and cradled her cheeks in his palms. "Just remember, if at any time you decide that you don't like my living here, you'll always have the option of kicking me out."

As she gazed up into his eyes, the real reason for her hesitancy suddenly struck her. She was just plain scared. And oddly enough, it wasn't so much the thought that he might curtail her independence that frightened her. No, she was afraid that Matt might reawaken the love that had died in her so long ago. Was she ready to risk being hurt again?

Yet, to have him in her bed every night, to wake

up beside him each morning . . . the temptation exceeded her doubts.

"So when do you want to move in?" she whispered, touching his hard jaw with her fingertips.

A slow smile lit up Matt's face. "You're sure about this?"

"Yes."

He lowered his lips to hers, murmuring, "Then how about we begin the arrangement right now?"

Chapter Nine

The early-morning sun splashed an oblong puddle of light onto the trestle table in the kitchen, illuminating the opened news magazine in front of Allison. The article she'd been scanning failed to hold her attention for long. She curled her fingers around a steaming mug of coffee, her eyes straying to the man sitting opposite her.

Matt's chair was at an angle to hers, his strong, handsome features profiled against the pine fireplace mantel behind him. He was studying the stock reports in the *Wall Street Journal*. In the burgundy flannel shirt and blue jeans he wore, he might have been mistaken for a laborer.

Crossing bare legs beneath her thick green bathrobe, Allison took a sip of coffee. Had it really only been two weeks since that Friday when she had agreed to let him move in with her? Her life had changed drastically in the interim. It was hard to remember how she had filled her evenings and weekends without Matt around to drag her off to an antique show or the Museum of Fine Arts in Boston or a day of cross-country skiing. Even when they stayed home, the air hummed with shared laughter and long discussions. And, oh, the nights!

Gazing at his rugged features, she felt a ghost of that familiar excitement stir deep inside her, an excitement he could fan into flames with just a smoldering look. On several occasions dinner had grown cold while they'd satisfied a more urgent hunger. And going to sleep with his arms wrapped around her had to be the sweetest experience in the world.

One thing was odd, though. She'd thought her desire would wane after a few weeks of living with him, but she only seemed to want him more and more. Still, she was realistic. This fever-pitch intensity couldn't last forever. So for the time being, she would simply enjoy his vitality, lovemaking, and companionship, all without the constraints and false promises of marriage.

The arrangement suited her far better than she'd thought it would. No one but Colleen knew they were living together, and Allison had sworn her sister to secrecy. If her parents suspected anything, they hadn't voiced any objections.

Allison sensed that Matt was making a special effort not to pressure her. Though he told her over and over how much he loved her, she was thankful that not once had he mentioned marriage again. Nothing he could say could induce her to give up her hard-won independence. And how deep and binding were his feelings anyway? She still found it hard to believe that he had loved her, really loved her, for so long and yet hadn't tried sooner to patch things up. Wouldn't he someday tire of her again, and dump her just as before?

And what did she feel for him? She frowned as she searched for words to describe the emotions he aroused in her. She felt buoyant and sparkling and fulfilled, but also wary and scared and uncertain. She felt satisfied, yet unsatisfied; contented, yet discontented; happy, yet unhappy. There was only one thing of which she was certain. She didn't want this enchanting interlude to end just yet.

Allison watched Matt pick up his coffee cup and take a sip, his eyes never leaving the tiny newsprint he was concentrating on. He was totally absorbed in the previous day's closing prices. With a prickling of concern, she studied the tired lines on his face. He had been working long hours over the past two weeks, often not getting home until seven or eight o'clock in the evening. On several occasions he'd had to drive into Boston for the day, and once he had stayed overnight to attend a board meeting early the next morning.

One of these days, he'll leave and never come back. Allison swallowed the dregs of her cold coffee, denying the raw fear that paralyzed her heart. *So what if he does? He can't hurt you this time.*

After all, their relationship was purely physical. Deliberately, she concentrated on cataloging the features in him which she found so attractive. The hard line of his jaw. The thick black hair with a few faint strands of silver, neatly trimmed so it just barely touched his collar. The amber eyes that could melt her with a single glance. The strong, lean fingers that could give such pleasure.

But he didn't belong to her, and he never would. Oh, dear God, why did she ache so whenever she thought of that? Was he beginning to mean more to her than she cared to admit?

Allison sprang to her feet, catching at the chair to keep from tripping on the hem of her bathrobe. Matt looked up from the newspaper as she steadied herself.

"I'm going to get myself some more coffee," she blurted, disciplining her emotions. "Would you like another cup?"

He glanced at his watch. "No, thanks. I've got to be going in a couple of minutes."

She walked to the counter for a refill, careful to avoid stepping on Louisa's kittens, which had just learned how to tumble out of the low box, eager to explore their new world. One of them, Allison noticed as she turned back around, was sprawled over Matt's shoe, batting at the lacing, hooking its paw in his sock. Matt calmly disengaged the tiny claws, then cuddled the bundle of gray fuzz against his chest.

"You'd better cool it, girl, before you get yourself in trouble," he told the little mewling creature.

"What makes you so sure that one's a girl?" Allison asked skeptically.

"Because she was trying to climb up my leg," he explained with a straight face. "All the ladies in this house just love to climb all over me."

"Is that a fact?" Allison put down her cup, coming

from behind to fold her arms around him. She kissed his cheek, smooth from recent shaving and smelling faintly of tangy cologne. "And whatever gave you that egotistical idea, hmm?"

"Why don't I just show you?"

Matt gently placed the kitten on the brick floor, letting it scamper off. Then he dragged Allison forward and tumbled her onto his lap. After looping her arms around his neck, he fused their mouths in a long, delicious kiss.

"Still think I'm being egotistical?" he murmured against her lips.

"Mmmm." She snuggled closer to him, hazy-eyed and lazy-limbed. "I can't make a judgment like that without gathering more evidence."

"Like this?"

Matt slid a hand inside the neckline of her bathrobe, curving his fingers around a warm, bare breast. His thumb stroked back and forth across the tip, and Allison sighed with pleasure.

A complacent grin creased his face. "How am I doing?"

"Don't stop," she implored, her voice husky and teasing. "I haven't quite made up my mind . . . Say, Matt?"

"Yes?" He bent and nuzzled her throat.

"Remember what you used to tell me?"

"When?"

"Back when we first started dating, and I used to worry that I wasn't . . . well, bustier?"

"Of course I remember." He chuckled as he lifted his head. " 'More than a handful is wasted.' "

"Don't laugh," she said, trying to be stern but not

quite succeeding. "Lots of girls are self-conscious about their breast size when they're growing up."

"Well, I've always thought you were just perfect." Matt gently stroked her breast, weighing the soft underside in his palm. He flashed her a wicked grin. "And now, after all that flattery, are you ready to agree that every female in this household is wild about me?"

Allison pretended to give it great consideration. "If I say yes, what's in it for me?"

He made an exaggerated leer. "Tonight I'll be yours to do whatever you want with, okay?"

"Why not right now?" she said, wiggling against him suggestively.

"Don't tempt me." With a look of regret, he pulled his hand out of her robe. "Much as I'd love to take you back to bed, I've got to get to work." He rose, letting her slide off his lap and onto her slippered feet.

"*Raawwk.* Good night," squawked Mr. Screech, prancing back and forth on the perch inside his brass cage by the hearth.

"That's good-bye, not good night," Allison corrected.

"Good night," the bird repeated, then added, "Cracker?"

"You can't reward him for his mistakes, then expect him to learn anything," Matt observed as she gave the parrot the requested saltine.

"He's a hopeless case, anyway," she rationalized.

"And you're a real soft touch when it comes to your pets. It's one of the many things I love about you."

They shared one last tender kiss before he headed out the door.

Later that morning, Allison sat at her drawing table, idly doodling on a sheet of paper. Though she knew she was building castles in the air, she couldn't help wondering what it would be like if her life with Matt never ended. Surely, she mused, it did little harm to spin such a fantasy—so long as she kept in mind that it was only a figment of her imagination.

Her eyes focused on the "Kit & Kaboodle" cartoon she had been drawing unconsciously, and dismay crossed her face. This morning she had begun a strip in which Stanley tries to convince Kit to marry him. Just as Stanley produces the engagement ring, the parrot Kaboodle was supposed to swoop down and swallow it. Instead, what she had penciled into the last frame was Kit throwing herself in Stanley's arms and accepting his marriage proposal!

Crumpling the paper in disgust, Allison flung it into the wastebasket. What had sparked such a sappy drawing, she didn't even want to try to guess. Diligently she started fresh, this time keeping to her original idea. When she finished inking it in an hour later, she gazed down at her handiwork in satisfaction. That was all she needed to complete for this week.

She picked up the stack of cartoons on her filing cabinet, added the new one to it, stuck them all between two pieces of cardboard, and then stuffed the whole lot into a large manila envelope, addressing the outside to the syndication company in New York that handled her strip.

Intending to go to the post office, Allison was pulling on her ski jacket when a sudden thought struck her. She glanced at her watch. Eleven-ten. What if, on her way back from mailing the envelope, she surprised Matt with lunch? She could stop at a deli in town and buy some sandwiches, then go out to the mill.

She finished her errands by noon, and headed for the mill. It was located a mile outside of town, and, as she drove, Allison hummed along with the tune playing on the radio, enjoying the white-frosted landscape. The day was crisp and cold and clear. The sun poured down over the woods on either side of the narrow road, throwing lacy tree shadows onto the snow. She couldn't remember a time when winter had sparkled so. Why was it that she had never before noticed what a beautiful season it was?

She was so busy admiring the scenery that she nearly missed the turnoff for the mill. Luckily there were no other cars around as she backed up and headed down the narrow road. Her BMW bumped along over the potholed surface, and for once Allison envied Matt his truck. She could understand why he didn't want to drive a Ferrari over this mess every day.

Off in the distance an enormous, sprawling, red-brick building loomed into view. There was a barbed-wire-topped chain-link fence around the property. The gate was wide open, and the small wooden guardhouse inside it was deserted.

Allison drove in, studying the large slate-roofed structure in front of her. Many of the windows were broken, and the whole place had an air of neglect.

Just beyond the mill, she caught a glimpse of the river. Dead brown reeds stuck up out of the snow to mark its shoreline.

There were several smaller brick buildings scattered to the right. Probably old dormitories, Allison guessed, relics of a time a century ago when the company had provided housing for its employees.

She saw Matt's truck in front of the main building. The only other vehicles in the parking lot were several vans from a local electrical company, a late-model Buick, and a pickup bearing the logo of Blair Building, the construction company owned by her brother-in-law, Joe, who had been contracted to help with the restoration.

Allison parked and walked toward the building, purse in one hand, paper sack of sandwiches in the other. Icy gusts of wind hustled her along over the patches of ice on the broken pavement. With a sigh of relief, she eased open the heavy wooden door and hurried inside. Though the interior wasn't much warmer, at least the chilly December breeze was gone.

She was standing in a long, wooden-floored hall that bisected the building. The wide doors on either side of her were open. Hearing the muted hum of voices coming from the right, Allison headed in that direction.

She stopped just inside the doorway, staring at the mammoth room. Rows of multipaned windows let in a watery sunlight through dirt-streaked glass. Whatever had once covered the walls had been torn off and hauled away, exposing the wooden beams beneath. At the far end of the room, there were four men in work clothes stringing electrical cable.

Looking to her left, she smiled. Matt was standing near the corner, his back to her. He wore a down vest over his burgundy shirt, and there was a white hardhat on his head. He was gesturing up at the ceiling while talking to her brother-in-law, a husky blond-haired man who stood several yards away.

Joe saw her and waved. He said something to Matt, who swiveled and started toward her, smiling. Joe was right behind him.

Just then, Allison heard an ominous cracking noise, and before she could even register what it was, she saw Matt pivot sharply with a swift glance upward.

He dived toward Joe, thrusting him aside in a tackle that knocked the brawny man off his feet. An instant later, a huge chunk of ceiling plaster slammed downward, the edge of it catching Matt and sending him sprawling to the floor in a shower of white dust.

Allison froze in horror. It seemed an eternity passed in which the only thing alive in her was the furious hammering of her heart. Overcome by a dread so deep and hideous that it paralyzed her limbs, all she could do for an instant was stare at Matt's unmoving form.

Then the purse and paper sack of sandwiches slid out of her numb fingers and she was running toward him, a prayer repeating over and over in her brain. *Oh, please, God, let him be all right. Let him be all right!*

By the time she was on her knees beside him, he was stirring. Joe got there just as she did. The crew of electricians who'd been working at the other end of the room came hurrying up right after them.

"Matt, are you okay?" she asked urgently, putting a light hand to his shoulder, almost afraid to touch him for fear he was injured.

"I think so," he said, sitting up carefully.

"Are you sure? You could have broken something," she persisted with a worried frown. "My car's out front—I'll drive you to the hospital."

"There's no need. Everything's in proper working order. See?" His voice calm and steady, Matt flexed his arms and fingers. "I was just stunned there for a minute."

"My God, you saved my life by knocking me out of the way like that," Joe said, his face pale. "That chunk would have hit me square on the head if you hadn't moved so quickly."

"Couldn't risk losing the best contractor in town, could I?" Matt said with a grin. He stood up, brushing off the white particles that clung to him. "At least this proved one thing."

"What's that?" asked Joe.

"We were right about the ceiling in the corner being unstable."

Joe laughed wryly. "You've got a point there—even if it was one hell of a way to find out."

Allison had gotten to her feet at the same time as Matt. Trembling from aftershock, she listened to the two men exchanging banter. How could they joke about it? Matt might have been killed! She pressed cold hands to her cheeks, unable to forget the image of his body lying motionless on the floor.

As if from a great distance, she heard Matt tell Joe and the others to take their lunch break. When they were gone, he put an arm around her shoulders.

"Well, it certainly is a pleasant surprise to see you

here," he said. "I'll bet you didn't expect such a dramatic reception."

Allison's laugh was strained. "That was some heroic deed you did there, pushing Joe out of the way."

"Pure instinct, not heroics," he said with a shrug. "Hey, you're shivering! Let's go over to my office—the heating system works over there."

His arm still around her, they walked outside and down a concrete path. A bitterly cold wind buffeted them, but Matt's body shielded her from the worst of it. A blast of warmth hit them as they entered a smaller brick building. They passed through a hall-way to an outer office furnished sparsely but tasteful-ly in blues and creams. The high, ornately plastered ceiling and intricate woodwork around the multi-paned windows gave the room a charm reminiscent of the nineteenth century. The secretary's desk was deserted.

"Agnes must be at lunch," Matt commented as they continued into his office.

He removed his hardhat and sent it sailing onto a chair, then walked to a large walnut desk strewn with papers. Allison glanced around in an effort to dis-tract herself. This room was clearly meant for work rather than a showplace for Matt to sit back and look important while others did the actual labor. In one corner was a round conference table surrounded by utilitarian straight-backed chairs. Tacked to the wall behind the table was an oversized architect's render-ing of the mill interior. The only piece of furniture designed strictly for comfort was a sofa in a nubby oatmeal fabric with a low coffee table in front of it.

Allison wandered to the window, the plush brown

carpeting muffling her footsteps. She looked out, seeing not the complex of buildings but Matt's unmoving body on the mill floor. The horror of it made her quake again despite the warmth of the air. She swallowed to ease the constriction in her throat.

"Well, Agnes left a note saying she'd be gone until two o'clock. That means we have an hour and a half to ourselves." Matt walked up behind her to slide his arms around her waist, fusing her spine to his hard chest. His fingers found the zipper to her jacket, pulling it down to allow him access to the soft swells of her breasts. "I hope you came here today wanting what's going through my mind right now," he murmured.

As he nuzzled her neck, Allison clamped her eyes shut to keep the mistiness in them from overflowing. She drew in a ragged breath, filling her lungs with his scent. It was an almost unbearably poignant experience to feel those vital hands caressing her when she might have lost him forever. Dear God, if he had been a split second slower out there in the mill . . .

She felt a tear spill down her cheek. It trickled into the corner of her mouth, tasting warm and salty. Allison gritted her teeth, trembling with the tension of maintaining control. Yet she was unable to prevent the slow, steady seepage as one droplet after another splashed downward.

"What . . . ?" Matt twisted her around to face him. "Honey, what's wrong? Why are you crying?"

"I'm not . . . I never cry," she choked out in denial.

But the perplexed, loving concern on his face made the dam burst. Rising from deep within her, a sob tore from her throat and a torrent of tears scalded her cheeks. She hid her face in her hands, feeling the barriers inside her being ripped away. It was the aftershock of the accident, she assured herself. But somehow she knew that that alone couldn't cause the aching desolation she felt whenever she thought about a life without him. He was bound to leave her; it was just a matter of time.

Matt nestled her against him, pressing her face to the down vest covering his chest. He was bewildered by her unexpected weeping. Was it his fault? Had he hurt her unknowingly? He thought over the past weeks, but came up empty-handed. Just this morning, they'd laughed and kissed like nothing was wrong. Was she developing feelings for him? It might not be love, but did he dare hope she at least cared for him, just a little?

Desperately, Allison clung to Matt as her anchor in the storm of tears. He was whispering soft words of empathy, his strong hands gentle as they stroked her hair. Oddly enough, despite her insecurities, his embrace made her feel protected.

Gradually the great, gut-wrenching sobs subsided, and sanity returned. Why had she let herself lose control like that? She was supposed to be a strong person! Ashamed, Allison kept her face buried against him, unwilling to meet his eyes. But Matt took her cheeks in his palms and urged her head up.

"Feel better now?"

She bit her lip, nodding shakily.

"Why don't you tell me what's bothering you." He guided her to the couch, pressing her down beside him, his arm around her.

"I'm . . . sorry," she stammered. "I . . . I haven't cried like that in years."

"There's no need to apologize."

She sniffed, swiping at her wet cheeks with her fingers. "I feel like a complete mess."

Matt smiled. "You must be feeling better if you're worrying about how you look." He dug in his hip pocket and produced a clean, folded handkerchief. "Here you go."

Allison accepted it gratefully and dried her eyes. Then, feeling awkward, she dropped her hands to her lap and stared down at the crumpled square of white linen.

"Tell me what's wrong," he prodded gently.

"I . . . it's silly. Can't we just forget it?"

His thumb and forefinger tipped her chin up. "It can't be silly if it made you cry like that."

His eyes were strangely watchful, his body tense. Allison knew she owed him an explanation. But it wasn't necessary to confess the part about not wanting him to leave her, was it?

"I . . . I guess it's just the shock of the accident," she said lamely. "Delayed reaction or something."

The stiffness in his shoulders relaxed as he let out a deep breath. "You were really that worried about me?"

She twisted the handkerchief. "It was awful, seeing you lying on the floor and not knowing whether you were dead or alive." To her consternation, Matt's face became a blur as the memory made tears mist her eyes again.

Pulling her to him, he combed his fingers into her hair. "Accidents happen now and then on any construction site. You shouldn't let it upset you."

"I know," she said, her voice muffled. "But

you've become a . . . a good friend, and I wouldn't want anything to happen to you."

"Nothing will," he said huskily. "Nothing is going to keep me from being with you and loving you."

She yearned to believe his promise. When their mouths met, Allison responded with shameless passion. There was some new depth to her need for him today, but she couldn't seem to focus on what it was; she knew only that she desperately wanted that special exhilaration she found only in his arms.

Matt pressed her into the cushions, his hand seeking the curve of her breast. Against her thigh she felt the hard evidence of his arousal. His expressive eyes blazed with an intensity that sent spasms of pleasure spiraling through her veins. His tongue tasted the sensitive surfaces inside her parted lips, his breath warm against her skin. She laced her fingers into his hair as desire set fire to her heart, searing all of her nerves.

He peeled off her jacket, then lifted the lavender sweater over her head, and removed her bra. The cool rush of air on her overheated skin brought back a measure of reason.

"Matt . . . the door. Someone might walk in."

"Everyone's at lunch. It's locked anyway."

His mouth dipped to the tip of one silky soft breast, his tongue teasing her until she was dizzy. He unzipped her jeans, his fingers delving inside to tantalize her. He was devastating her senses. Her throat arched back, her hair splashing across the cushions like filaments of fire.

Trembling, she sought his shirt buttons. She wanted to be a part of him, to please him as he was pleasing her. She let herself pretend that they had a real chance to make a life together, that Matt would never, ever leave her. Gently he aided her in stripping away the rest of their clothing. Then he lowered himself onto her.

"Oh, God, Allison, I love you so much!"

The raspy growl of his voice was music to her ears. If only she could believe his words! She strained upward, relishing the slightly abrasive texture of his chest hair against her tender breasts. Matt kissed the pulse that raced in her throat. His fingers drifted downward, roving over her silken belly and lower, finding the moist, most intimate secrets of her body, caressing her until she writhed with wild arousal.

With one strong thrust he entered her. Her blood pounded with the pleasure of it; she felt giddy with bliss at surrendering her whole being to him. They were one person, one body, one soul. She tucked her face in his neck, tasting the salt of his skin, her hips lifting to meet his. Need pulsed through her, growing and building until she was released, shaken, and clinging to Matt.

For long moments, they lay unmoving, reluctant to return to reality. Opening her eyes, Allison saw Matt smiling down at her. His gaze was alive with tenderness as he ran a finger down her flushed cheek.

"What do you say we spend the rest of the afternoon right here?" he suggested with a devilish leer.

"With your secretary sitting a few feet outside this office? No way."

"Come on, I can tell Agnes I'm in conference and don't want to be disturbed."

"All afternoon?"

"Why not?" He cupped a rosy-tipped breast in his palm. "I'll just tell her it's an extremely important conference."

"And you plan to conduct said conference entirely in body language, huh?" Allison teased. "When I came to see you, all I wanted was to bring you lunch but . . . oh!" Abruptly she squirmed out from under him. "Matt, I just remembered! I must have dropped my things over in the mill! I brought you your favorite sandwich, corned beef on rye with lots of mustard. I hope no one stole it!" She hopped off the sofa and grabbed her lace panties from the floor.

"There go my plans for the afternoon. You're more interested in food than me," Matt grumbled as he got up. "I suppose you even expect me to do the gentlemanly thing and go get the stuff for you."

She wound her arms around his neck, dangling her undies down his back. "My, how perceptive of you."

"You think I'm doing this out of the goodness of my heart? Wait till you find out what my payment terms are." He gave her a lusty smack on the behind, then pulled on his clothes.

When he was gone, Allison finished dressing and plopped back down on the sofa, leaning her head against the cushions. A dreamy look flitted over her face. No man but Matt had ever made her feel this sense of completeness. He was all male, that complementing half of her which she hadn't known was missing from her life. There was more, so much more, to their relationship than mere sexual attraction.

With sudden shattering force, the truth struck her.

The pleasure faded from her expression, and her palms broke out in a cold sweat. She tried to tell herself that she was mistaken; she would never be that much of a fool. But the words scorching her brain could not be denied.

She was in love with him.

Chapter Ten

*H*ey, Alli, guess what?" Allison had no chance to reply as Colleen's voice rattled on excitedly over the telephone line. "Joe stopped by today! We were planning to go out tonight since it's my night off, but he said he just couldn't wait that long to see me. Well, he came right to the point and said he loves me and hates living apart from me and the kids. And so we decided it was time he moved back home! It's a good thing I'd arranged for the twins to stay overnight with Mom and Dad, because I've got a real romantic night planned—champagne and soft music and everything. Isn't it wonderful?"

"But I thought you wanted to be independent for a while."

"Of course," Colleen agreed. "I'm still going to take some college classes and then open my own restaurant someday. But my career isn't as important as my marriage."

"Aren't you afraid that Joe might walk out on you again sometime?" Allison persisted.

"I suppose that's a possibility if we don't work at communicating. But I guess you have to be willing to take a chance if you really love someone."

Long after her sister had hung up, Allison pondered Colleen's words, applying them to her own relationship with Matt. Why was it that Colleen could so easily forgive and forget while she herself found it impossible to take that risk with Matt?

She began preparing beef Stroganoff for supper, her mind only half on the task. Six days had passed since that bittersweet moment when she had realized she still loved Matt. The acknowledgment had stunned her, yet she was aware of a certain crazy, irrepressible joy, too. More than anything else in the world she wanted to believe that he really loved her, that his feelings weren't as shallow as she feared. The way she was growing more and more dependent on him frightened her.

Allison drew in a deep breath of pine-scented air, her eyes filling with tears as they focused on the wreath that hung on the back door. Christmas was a week away. How much longer did she have with Matt? Another month? Half a year? How long before he tired of her again?

Yes, her problems with Matt were far more complicated than Colleen had experienced with Joe, Allison concluded as she sautéed mushrooms for the Stroganoff. He had broken off their engagement twelve years ago without even trying to work things out. She could finally accept that they had both been too young, and that the financial problems of his family's business had put pressure on him. Yet surely those two reasons alone shouldn't have made him forsake his vow to cherish her forever. Unless he hadn't really loved her deeply in the first place.

That would explain why his parents had so easily influenced him, Allison thought as she added strips of beef to the mushrooms, wine, and spices in the pan. She frowned, remembering the Christmas party Matt's mother was giving on the coming Saturday night, to which they had been invited. To be more specific, she corrected cynically, Matt and *a date* had been invited.

She was certain Mrs. Wakefield meant for him to bring someone suitable, a woman from a background similar to his own. After all, he was a Boston blue blood who could trace his roots to British nobility, whereas her own ancestors had been poor Irish immigrants. Since Allison hadn't been good enough for Matt years ago, there was no reason to think his mother had changed her mind in the interim.

Despite her self-confidence in other areas, she experienced a queasy stomach and damp palms at the thought of facing Mrs. Wakefield and her snooty society friends. She wanted to crawl into a hole and hide until the party was all over. It was silly, she told herself, but she couldn't get rid of a gut feeling of inferiority. So what if she had money now. That alone wouldn't make her acceptable. Yet pride had forced her to agree to attend the party anyway. She would never let his mother see just how intimidated she really was.

Allison was putting the noodles on to boil when

she heard the distant rattle and slam of the front door. Another faint clattering. Matt was hanging up his coat. A soft click as the closet door was shut. Out in the hall, Winston's claws clacked on the bare pine floor along with the familiar male footsteps that approached the kitchen.

She couldn't help smiling as she stirred the noodles. It was the same pattern every evening. The knowledge that Matt had come home to her gave her a warm feeling inside, like the security of a routine as dependable as the sunset and the rising of the moon. Her pleasure faded, and she put the spoon down to fold her arms across her breasts. Oh, why couldn't this enchanting interlude last forever?

Matt's large hands spanned her waist. "Hi, honey. I hope you missed me today as much as I missed you."

He parted her hair to kiss her nape. Allison leaned back to drink in the feel of his strong body against her spine, then she twirled in his embrace and gave him a fierce hug.

"I'm glad you're home," she whispered huskily. She buried her face in his flannel shirt, breathing in his heady scent.

"Now that's the kind of welcome I like."

Cradling her cheeks in his palms, Matt lifted her face to his kiss. His lips carried a trace of cold from the outdoors but swiftly warmed as they explored her mouth with mesmerizing pressure. Allison tangled her fingers into the thickness of his hair. Loving Matt was both joy and agony. Not even the certainty of greater pain when their relationship inevitably ended seemed to prevent her from falling deeper and deeper under his spell. And each day it became more tempting to once again commit her life to him.

But that would be the height of folly.

She wrenched herself away, resisting the lure of his body. "Dinner's going to be ruined if we keep this up," she said shakily.

Matt flashed her a half-smile. "That's never stopped us before."

"But . . ." Allison fumbled for an excuse when all she wanted was to fling herself back into his arms. "The noodles for the Stroganoff are about to over-cook."

He grinned. "Heaven forbid that such a tragedy should happen. All right, I give up . . . but only until later."

He set the table while Allison finished preparing dinner. As they ate, Matt gave her an update on the progress at the mill. She in turn told him about a call she'd gotten from the syndication company that morning. A publisher was interested in putting to-gether a book of collected "Kit & Kaboodle" car-toons. It wasn't until they were finishing a dessert of peach cobbler that she brought up the topic of Colleen and Joe getting back together.

"I'm glad she's happy again." Allison couldn't help a sigh as she stared down at her coffee cup. She wished she could be as lucky in love as her sister. Why had she fallen for a man who couldn't be trusted?

"Then why the sad face?" Matt asked softly. "If they love each other enough, things will work out for them."

He thought she was worried about Colleen's relationship! "How can you be sure of that?" she asked, preferring to keep the spotlight on her sister rather than having him guess her true concern.

"Because I'm a strong believer in the power of love." Matt reached across the table and took her hand, his thumb stroking the sensitive skin of her palm. "How else could I go on living here with you if I didn't have the hope that someday you might learn to love me as much as I love you?"

The depth of feeling in his amber eyes almost made her blurt out the words she knew he was waiting to hear. Allison bit back the impulse.

"When are you going to realize that you're wasting your time?" she said coolly, jerking her hand free.

The light in his gaze was suddenly shuttered. "It's not a waste of time."

"Yes, it is. Like I've said before, Matt, all I want from you is an affair."

"You might change your mind."

"You'd best have a lot of patience, then. You've got a long wait ahead of you." She pushed back her chair and grabbed her plate, marching over to the counter.

"Allison."

Her name was a half-tender, half-exasperated sigh on his lips as Matt came from behind, looping his arms around her. The dish slipped from her fingers and clattered into the sink. She stiffened her spine to keep from melting into the inviting warmth of his body.

"Let's not argue, sweetheart," he murmured into her hair. "Let's not worry about the future at all. I'm sorry I even brought up the topic." One of his hands strayed to her breast, brushing its fullness through her sweater. "I'd rather make love to you than get into a pointless argument. What do you say we go upstairs and—"

"No!" Allison twisted free. With her emotions as shaky as they were at the moment, she knew it was best to avoid making love where she would be so vulnerable. "I . . . I promised to drop off a box of toys tonight to a needy family in town," she fibbed. In reality, she had planned on doing that tomorrow.

"I'll drive you."

"That isn't necessary. Besides, I fixed dinner, so it's your turn to do the dishes."

"They'll keep until we get back."

Allison glared at him. "I'm going alone."

"Not if I have anything to say about it," he warned in a voice that brooked no argument. "You're not gallivanting around town alone after dark in God only knows what kind of neighborhood."

"I can take care of myself."

"If you try to go without me, I'll just follow you."

"Oh . . . suit yourself, then." Abruptly she gave in, knowing that if she didn't, he would do precisely as he said.

Allison turned on her heel and stalked out of the kitchen, nearly tripping over Winston. The dog had gotten into the habit of sleeping in the hall in front of the doorway, since it was barred from the kitchen while Louisa and the kittens were there. Matt grabbed her elbow to steady her, and she thought she heard him chuckle softly.

She jerked away and stormed down to the front closet. Damn him anyway! she fumed as she yanked on her ski jacket. Couldn't he take a hint that she needed some time alone? But no, he always had to boss her around.

"We'll take my truck," Matt announced as they went out into the crisp, cold night.

They stopped at the community center to pick up the box of used toys, which had been donated in a drive sponsored by several local church groups. For the past few years, Allison had made a habit of volunteering an afternoon each week to helping out those less fortunate than herself. She found it far more satisfying than simply writing out a check and letting someone else do the work. Not to mention that she had met many interesting people in the process.

She directed Matt into a poorer section of town, near the river. The streets were narrow here, the houses small and jammed together. Behind one home, Allison caught a glimpse of someone's laundry hanging stiff in the icy air. There was a general air of shabbiness and decay. Across the dirty snow, the wind whipped a section of newspaper, rolling and tossing it like a bit of urban tumbleweed.

Matt pulled up at the address she gave him, parking beneath a dim streetlight. He got the box out of the rear of the truck and followed her up a cracked concrete walk leading to a minuscule frame house. As they drew nearer, it was plain that the owners were meticulous about keeping up the appearance of their home. Though the paint on the woodwork showed signs of peeling, the porch had been neatly swept. Clean but threadbare curtains hung inside the lighted, freshly washed windows.

A thin young man with receding brown hair answered their knock. "Hello, Allison," he exclaimed. "This is a surprise! We weren't expecting you until tomorrow. Come on in."

As they entered, Allison caught Matt's shrewd glance, which plainly said: *So you'd planned to visit tonight, did you?* She felt her cheeks redden from more than just the icy weather.

After handing Rob their coats, they went into a tiny living room where an elderly woman in a wheelchair sat with an afghan over her lap. She raised sightless brown eyes to the doorway.

"Rob, who's there?" she asked in a cracked, aged voice.

"It's just me, Mrs. Morgan," Allison said, answering for her grandson.

"Allison, my dear! Come over and say hello." Mrs. Morgan's wrinkled face broke into a smile as she held out a blue-veined hand. "There's someone here with you, isn't there? A man, I believe."

"I can't ever hide anything from you, can I?" Allison said, laughing as she grasped the woman's frail fingers. "How did you know?"

"Just because I'm blind doesn't mean I've lost my other senses, dearie. I heard his footsteps, and I can smell just a trace of his cologne. Well, don't keep me in suspense; introduce us!"

"He's Matt Wakefield, a friend of mine. Matt, this is Mrs. Morgan and her grandson, Rob."

Matt had put down the box of toys in a corner. He shook hands with Rob, then walked over and took the old woman's other hand. "I'm pleased to meet you, Mrs. Morgan."

"Ah, I was beginning to wonder if Allison would ever bring a young man to visit along with her. Tell me, dearie, is he as handsome as his voice sounds?"

"Oh, yes," she blurted. Her heart lurched at Matt's smile, and she quickly changed the subject. "I . . . we just stopped by to drop off some toys for the children." She added, to Matt, "Rob has three little girls, ages two, four, and five."

"We really appreciate this," said Rob. "The kids are in bed, but I'm going to hide these toys just in case they wake up. I'll wrap everything later so they'll have something to open on Christmas."

"I can't tell you how wonderful Allison has been to us," Mrs. Morgan said to Matt as her grandson left the room with the box. "She's been a big help since Rob's wife passed away last summer. Rob was laid off from his job at about the same time, and we didn't think we'd be able to provide much of a Christmas for the girls this year. Now, thanks to Allison, they'll have a happy one."

"It's the community center you should be grateful to, not me," Allison protested.

"There's no need to be so humble, dearie," chided the old woman. "Now I've got something for you, too. Could you fetch me my sewing kit? I think I left it over there." She pointed a knobby finger to a blue sofa against the wall.

"Of course." Obediently, Allison got the basket for her.

"It's right here on top." Mrs. Morgan felt around in the basket, pulling out a tissue-wrapped package and holding it up.

Allison stripped away the paper to find a set of white place mats crocheted in fine, delicate yarn.

"They're exquisite," she admired. She was all the more touched because Mrs. Morgan usually sold her handiwork at a little boutique in town. Allison was tempted to refuse the gift because she knew how badly the family needed the extra money. Yet she couldn't bear to hurt Mrs. Morgan's pride. Overcome by emotion, she bent and kissed the woman's cheek. "Thank you so very much."

"You do lovely work, Mrs. Morgan," Matt added softly. "It's amazing, considering you can't see what you're doing."

Allison stiffened, hoping Mrs. Morgan wouldn't be offended by his reference to her blindness. But the old woman seemed pleased by his directness.

"I may not be able to see, but I can feel. Believe it or not, these old hands of mine are very sensitive," she explained, wiggling her thin fingers. "My only regret is that I'm a little slow. It took me several months to finish that gift for Allison's hope chest."

"You mean my hopeless chest," Allison joked nervously.

"Now that's no way to talk," Mrs. Morgan scolded. "Tell me, Mr. Wakefield, don't you think Allison will make some lucky man a wonderful wife?"

"Call me Matt," he said, putting a gentle hand on the aging woman's shoulder. "And yes, you're right about Allison. As a matter of fact, I'm trying to talk her into marrying me."

"I knew it," Mrs. Morgan crowed, her face beaming. "We'll soon be hearing wedding bells."

Allison glared at Matt. But despite her annoyance, her knees weakened at the warmth in his eyes. She fought the treacherous softening. She would never make the mistake of marrying him, and anyway, he had no right to broadcast their private differences.

"Mrs. Morgan," she began firmly, "Matt and I are not—"

She was interrupted when Rob walked back into the room. "Sorry I was gone so long, folks, but I needed to check on the girls. Can I get anyone a cup of coffee or something?"

"I'm sure Allison and her young man are anxious to be off to spend some time alone with each other," said Mrs. Morgan.

"That's not true," Allison protested.

"Now, dearie, you can't fool an old fool like me," Mrs. Morgan said with a smile. "I remember what it was like to be in love. You two run along. You can come back another day and visit."

"You're an astute woman," Matt said, chuckling. "I'm pleased to have met you." He kissed her frail hand.

Mrs. Morgan blushed like a girl. "Oh, go on with you. We can chat another time."

"But—" Allison began.

"Thanks for everything," Matt cut in. "That's a lovely set of place mats you made." He squeezed Allison's arm, as if she needed a reminder, she thought resentfully.

Swallowing a retort, she agreed, "They're beautiful, and I'll always treasure them, Mrs. Morgan. We really don't have to leave so quickly, though—"

But Matt was already towing her to the front door. Rob followed, getting their coats from the hall closet. Allison fumed in silence as the two men spoke.

"So you haven't been able to find a job anywhere in town?" Matt asked.

Rob shook his head in dejection. "With the economy the way it is, no one is hiring. During the summer, I did some yard work, but at this time of year, even that's impossible."

"If you're willing to work some late hours, I might be able to help."

A spark of hope shone in Rob's eyes. "I'd do just about anything. What did you have in mind?"

"We can discuss it tomorrow, if you'll come out to my mill."

"Oh, so you're *that* Wakefield," Rob exclaimed with dawning awe. At Matt's nod, he added, "Gee, I didn't make the connection at first. Everyone in town has been talking about how you're fixing up the old place."

"I take it you know your way out there, then."

"You bet! I can be there first thing in the morning."

"I'll see you then," Matt said.

When they were in the truck headed for home, Allison couldn't hold back her resentment any longer. "We could have stayed longer," she said stiffly.

"I know that." Matt glanced at her through the gloomy interior. "But it made Mrs. Morgan happy to think of our being alone with each other. Anyway, she was right. I would like to spend some time with you tonight."

"And what about what *I* want?"

"Hopefully, it's the same thing I do."

"And if it isn't?" she retorted, beyond caring that she was being childish.

He threw her an impatient look. "What's eating

you tonight, anyway? Why don't you get it out and be done with it?"

"All right, then." Allison was spoiling for a fight, tired of bottling up her emotional turmoil, wanting to lash out at the man who had turned her life upside down. "How about if we start with Rob? I hope you haven't given him false expectations with that job offer. He's had a lot of hard knocks lately, and he doesn't need to have you go back on your word."

"Is that the kind of man you think I am?" Matt asked bitterly, his hands tightening around the steering wheel.

"I can only judge by my own experience. You made a vow to never leave me; then you took off at the first sign of trouble. That tells me you don't keep your promises."

"How long are you going to continue to crucify me for a mistake I made when I was only eighteen?" he demanded harshly. "I told you the circumstances behind our breakup. I believed I was doing what was best for you."

"Best for me? Or best for you and your parents?"

She saw his lips compress as he gazed through the windshield into the darkness illuminated by the truck's headlights. They had left town and were heading down the winding country road that led to Allison's house.

"Leave my parents out of this." There was a taut control to his voice, as if he were just barely keeping his temper in check. "Whether they were involved or not at some point makes absolutely no difference now."

"It does when I have to face your mother at that party on Saturday," Allison insisted, her fingers digging into the fragile fabric of the place mats. "With the way she feels about me, it's going to be mighty awkward seeing her."

"My mother never disliked you," he countered. "As a matter of fact, she was thrilled when I told her that you and I were seeing each other again."

"Don't lie to me, Matt."

"You don't have a whole hell of a lot of trust in anything I say, do you?" he snapped bitterly.

"Can you blame me?" she shot back.

He made no reply, and there was stony silence for the remainder of the ride. Arguing accomplished nothing, Allison thought wearily as they entered the house; they only seemed to go in circles. Venting her anger left her with more of a feeling of despair than ever. Quickly she ran up to the bedroom before he could see the tears that filled her eyes.

In bleak silence, Matt watched her ascend the stairs. He knew he ought to go after her, but he was still too furious. More than that, though, he was hurt, he admitted.

He strode into the library and lit up a cigarette, prowling restlessly around the antique-filled room. He'd be the first to agree that he deserved a kick in the teeth for the way he'd treated her so long ago. But hadn't he paid for his mistake in the anguish he'd felt, and then in those lonely years without her?

Dammit, he was beginning to think she'd never trust him again. He wondered for the hundredth time if he ought to tell her the truth about his mother's part in their breakup, but decided against it. Allison had a mental roadblock when it came to his mother. After the Christmas party, when she'd had a chance to see for herself that his mother held no grudge against her, then maybe Allison would be ready to hear the whole story.

Matt blew out a thin stream of smoke, fighting a dark hopelessness. Had it been a mistake to move in with her? At the time, it had seemed like an inspired compromise. But now, after three weeks of living with her, he realized that he had fallen more deeply in love, when all she'd given him in return was her body.

Could she ever love him again? He frowned. Before tonight, he could have sworn there had been a softening in her attitude toward him. Maybe he'd only been deluding himself, though, seeing things that weren't there because he wanted so badly to believe in them.

With sudden savagery, Matt ground out his cigarette in an ashtray. Who was he fooling? She didn't want marriage or a family; she was too independent to need anyone.

He knew he ought to cut his losses and leave, but instead he was going to walk up those stairs and try once more. No matter how much she was using him, he couldn't face the thought of living without her, not when he'd just found her again.

Chapter Eleven

The sleek red sports car shot through the darkness like a bullet. Allison shifted in the luxurious leather seat, her senses attuned to the silent man at the wheel beside her. Since Matt had had business in Boston yesterday, he had left his Bronco there in favor of his Ferrari. Very politely he had explained that he was sure she would prefer to go to his mother's Christmas party in something classier than a truck.

Allison stared out into the night and sighed, her breath condensing like fog on the cold window. She wished there were something she could do to ease the strain between them that had sprung up after that argument two days ago. Yet how could she retract what she had said to him when it was the unfortunate truth? She didn't trust him. That was precisely why she couldn't tell him that she loved him.

And ever since, their relationship had been little more than an armed truce. Treating each other warily, they had by tacit agreement ignored that brief, wretched confrontation. But it hadn't been forgotten. It loomed between them like some malignant growth, tainting the air and poisoning their friendship. Even their lovemaking had been tinged with a bittersweet poignancy, as if they were both grasping at a happiness which forever eluded them.

She stole a glance at Matt's profile. The chiseled angles of his face were illuminated by the ghostly light of the instrument panel. His brooding, introspective mood matched her own. She had never felt so keenly the hopelessness of their situation.

Matt's large hands grasped the steering wheel with competent ease. The expert tailoring of his tuxedo emphasized his muscular build. Somehow his formal attire made him seem different, more remote and out of her reach. Tonight he was Matthew Clayton Wakefield III, scion of a wealthy, powerful family. He belonged at the party they were going to. She didn't.

Dread clawed at Allison's stomach as they entered the outskirts of Boston. She was in no mood to deal with his mother's disapproval. If it hadn't been for a crazy desire to prove that she couldn't be intimidated, she would have stayed home tonight, letting Matt attend the party by himself.

Nervously she plucked at her long skirt. Was she dressed elegantly enough to meet the cream of Boston society? Back home, she had been pleased with her appearance. Her lacy white blouse had accentuated her fragile features, the taffeta skirt in dark reds and greens shot through with gold thread had looked stylish. But now she had doubts. Of course, her fox jacket and upswept hair added a chic touch, but . . .

Oh, hell! Here she was, a mature woman of twenty-nine, and she was letting herself feel threatened by a herd of old ladies who had never done a lick of real work in their lives. What did they have to be proud of besides a fate which had put a silver spoon into their mouths at birth? At least she had accomplished something by using her creative talent and drive. She had become one of the few success stories in a field where thousands had tried and failed to reach the top.

Resolutely Allison stared out the window at the city lights streaking past. Matt smoothly shifted gears, guiding the Ferrari into that bastion of influence and old money known as Beacon Hill, located adjacent to the Boston Common. He parked between a Mercedes and a Jaguar on a crowded, sloping street lined by elegant row houses. As they got out to stroll down the brick sidewalk, Allison frowned.

"This isn't the street where your parents used to live," she remarked, remembering the stately four-storied mansion she had visited so long ago.

"Their house was several blocks away. After my father died, mother moved because the place was too big for just her."

"You weren't staying with her?"

"No, I own a house off Louisburg Square. Mother and I both found it . . . simpler if we lived apart."

So you could entertain women in the privacy of

your own home? Allison longed to ask. She shivered, unprepared for the jealousy that jolted her heart. Slipping her hands into the pockets of her fur, she squinted up at the fat snowflakes drifting down from the dark sky. Why should it matter how many other women he had slept with?

Mrs. Wakefield's home was easy to spot as a chauffeured limousine glided to a halt in front to let its glittering occupants emerge into the chilly night air. The three-story row house was ablaze with light, the portico festooned with holiday greenery. Flanking the door were matching leaded glass panels, and above was a Georgian fan-light window.

Allison drew in a deep breath to quell her jittery nerves as she walked up the granite steps with Matt. His hand lightly rested on the fox jacket covering her back. She gleaned little comfort from his nearness, her mind leaping to the ordeal ahead. They slipped inside just behind a haughty-looking elderly couple. A white-coated servant closed the door behind them and politely took Allison's wrap.

The small entrance hall was crammed with people, the air heavy with the smell of expensive perfumes. The decor had the same subtle elegance as the exterior of the house. There was a marble floor in a checkerboard of black and white, and the walls were covered in a delicate cream-colored paper. The wide, curving staircase was flanked by a mahogany balustrade in the Chinese Chippendale style.

Matt slowly propelled her through the guests with a guiding hand on her elbow, heading toward an open double doorway to the right. Allison's eyes widened as she spotted Matt's mother through a break in the milling guests. Time hadn't altered those aristocratic features; Regina Wakefield still had the same high cheekbones, the regal uptilt to the chin, the haughty brown eyes that had always seemed so judgmental. Yet now she looked so . . . *old*. Shocked, Allison studied the woman. Her once black hair had turned white, and the reed-slender body in the rose silk gown appeared to be frail almost to the point of gauntness.

An unexpected wave of compassion swept over Allison, but she brushed it aside impatiently. Why was she feeling any pity for Matt's mother after the way the woman had looked down on her? *You can never be too rich or too thin.* Undoubtedly, Regina Wakefield ascribed to that adage and purposely dieted to attain a stylish svelteness. And of course she looked old. She'd had her only child late in life, and was now at least seventy.

Laughter and muted conversation spilled into the entrance hall as Allison and Matt approached Mrs. Wakefield, who was standing at the doorway to the drawing room, greeting her guests. "Hello, mother," he said, bending to kiss her cheek.

"Why, Matthew, darling, I'm glad you were able to come."

"I've brought someone with me. You remember Allison O'Shea, don't you?"

Allison had been hanging back, and Matt applied subtle but firm pressure to her waist to urge her forward. With a wooden smile she stepped closer and grasped Mrs. Wakefield's outstretched hands. The elderly woman's skin felt cool and fragile beneath her fingers.

"Of course I remember you, Allison," Regina Wakefield said. "It's wonderful to see you again." Her mouth was curved into a gentle, reserved smile.

"It's nice to see you too. You . . . have a lovely home." Allison forced out the platitude, unable to think of anything else to say.

"Why, thank you."

"Hello, Milton," Matt said, shaking the hand of a portly man at his mother's side.

"Oh, please forgive me," Regina broke in quickly. "I haven't introduced you, Allison. This is Milton Baxter, my physician and very dear friend. Milton, this is Allison O'Shea."

"How do you do?" Allison said, shaking the man's proferred hand. Dr. Baxter was a jolly-looking man in his sixties. He had a polished skull with only the merest fringe of silvering brown hair, giving him a monkish appearance despite his formal black tuxedo.

"Milton has been so kind and patient to stand here with me," said Regina with a fond smile at her companion. "He simply refuses to listen when I tell him he should go enjoy himself with the other guests."

"How could I enjoy myself any more than I already am?" Dr. Baxter said gallantly. "I'm with the most beautiful lady at the party, aren't I?"

"You old flatterer." Regina's eyes glittered with amusement. "You think if you appeal to my vanity, I'll change my mind. But I insist that you go have some fun, and I won't take no for an answer."

Allison caught the two men exchanging a swift, guarded glance. Then Matt said, "Milton, why don't you take Allison on in. I'll stay here with mother."

"I don't need a baby-sitter," Regina protested.

Matt left Allison to put an arm around his mother's thin shoulders. "Of course you don't. But I haven't seen you in several weeks, and this way we'll have some time together."

"Well, all right," Regina relented. "Oh . . . Allison, I hope we'll have a chance to chat later on." There was an almost hesitant quality to her cultured voice, but Allison dismissed it. She was imagining things. Regina Wakefield was only mouthing polite words like any proper lady and didn't really mean what she said.

With an uneasy glance at Matt, Allison let Dr. Baxter take her by the arm and lead her into the drawing room. Though she maintained an outward poise, she felt nervous inside as they threaded through the crowd. All the women here looked so sophisticated. Were any of them Matt's ex-lovers?

Gathering her pride, Allison lifted her chin. No one would ever know how intimidated she really was. Assuming an air of cosmopolitan indifference, she surveyed her surroundings.

The long room was designed for entertaining, and extended from the front of the house to the rear. Several cozy seating arrangements encouraged the formation of intimate groups. Garlands of greenery were draped over an Adam-style mantel, and a fire burned merrily in the hearth. In a bow window facing the street, twinkling with tiny white lights and festooned with red ribbons, was a huge Christmas tree. Stationed beside it was a quartet of musicians, and the soft strains of holiday music drifted through the air.

As they made their way through the throng,

Allison couldn't help noticing the valuable antiques scattered throughout the room. A Ming vase here, a grouping of Staffordshire figures there, a Belgian tapestry dominating a wall. Much of it was too rich for her own taste, but the artist in her could still appreciate the masterful mixture of textures and colors.

They sat down on an unoccupied sofa. Beyond the French windows spanning the back wall was a small terrace. Its sole occupants were a man and woman who were embracing, oblivious to the snowflakes floating down around them. They gazed into each other's eyes, their mutual adoration etched in sharp profile by a lighted lantern perched on a wrought-iron table. Allison glanced away from the intimate scene, aware of a poignant ache deep within her. Why couldn't she and Matt find such joy?

"I hope you don't mind my dragging you all the way back here," Dr. Baxter said. "But I thought it would be less crowded and quieter."

"Of course I don't mind. Look, Dr. Baxter," she added awkwardly, "you don't have to bother with me, really you don't. I know you have friends here you'd probably rather—"

"Call me Milton," he interrupted, giving her a kindly pat on the arm. "And most of my friends are old fogies like myself. It isn't often that I have the undivided attention of a pretty young lady like you."

"You're not an old fogy, Milton," Allison protested. "But thanks for looking out for me anyway. I'm afraid I don't know any of these people here."

"I'll be happy to introduce you in a moment." He lifted two glasses of champagne from a silver tray offered by a passing servant, handing one to Allison.

"For now, though, I wonder if you'd satisfy an old man's curiosity. Excuse me for being blunt, but you were engaged to Matthew once, weren't you?"

"Yes, but how did you . . ."

"I've known Regina for years. She's usually very close-mouthed when it comes to private family matters, but she did tell me the bare bones of the story just after it happened. I remember how . . . upset she was over the whole matter."

Yes, I'll bet she was. Aloud, Allison said, "Well, that's all in the past now."

Milton took a sip of champagne, watching her thoughtfully. "Yet you're here at the party with Matthew. Perhaps that means there's still something between the two of you?"

"No."

"But I believe perhaps you're still in love with him, are you not?"

Those shrewd eyes wouldn't let her voice the denial that leaped to her lips. She took a deep breath to ease the tautness in her throat, then admitted, "Yes."

"I can see you think I'm meddling in something which is none of my business," he stated with a patient smile. "Believe me, I'm only concerned for Regina's sake. She's not in the best of health, and I wouldn't like to see anything happen that might cause her distress."

"I understand."

Allison's fingers tightened around the delicate stem of her glass as she looked out the French windows. The lovers were gone from the terrace now; only soft, silent snowflakes sifted through the frosty night air. Yes, she understood Milton's unspo-

ken message, she thought dismally. He knew as well
as she how appalled Regina Wakefield would be if
her son were to make the mistake of marrying out of
his social class. She could at least reassure the doctor
that his fears were ungrounded.

"You can tell Mrs. Wakefield that she has absolutely nothing to worry about," Allison said, forcing
a bright smile toward her companion.

"I'm glad to hear that. Matthew's a good man,
and he deserves only the best." Milton set his empty
glass on a table and stood up, offering her his hand.
"Now, how about if we make the rounds, as I
promised we would?"

Her taffeta skirt rustled as they walked over to
join a cluster of people near the fireplace. Milton
introduced her to a grizzled old man who turned out
to be the owner of a renowned art gallery; a young
blond woman with a sweet face who cheerfully
announced to anyone who would listen that she was
celebrating the one-week anniversary of her divorce;
and a bald lawyer who would have talked Allison's
ear off about his passion for orchid-growing, had
Milton not rescued her.

As she and Milton moved from group to group,
Allison met people in occupations ranging from
ballet to business. She began to relax more, enjoying
the opportunity to study the diverse characters with
an artist's eye. Only two guests were rude. One was
a diamond-decked matron with a mouth that looked
like she'd just bitten into a lemon, and the other was
a stork-legged model who seemed to reserve her
smiles for men only.

Milton finally excused himself, explaining that he
needed to talk to Regina. The party was not quite

what she had expected, Allison reflected with surprise as a servant refilled her glass of champagne. Perhaps she had been wrong in believing that she would never fit into Matt's world.

Pretending to listen to a debate two women were having over the merits of several interior designers, she thought back to what Milton had said about Matt. *He deserves only the best.* The doctor had, of course, been referring to a wife with the proper bloodlines. She couldn't take offense at his words, because she knew he only meant to be kind. He was both protecting Regina Wakefield's interests and warning Allison herself against getting more deeply involved lest she be hurt.

She took a swallow of champagne, fighting a wretched wave of misery. If tonight was any indication, Matt was already losing interest. Only once in the past hour and a half had he sought her out, and then he had spoken but a few words to her before leaving again.

Sipping champagne, Allison let her eyes drift over the crowded room in an unconscious search for him. She stiffened when she saw him. He was leaning a shoulder against a wall, engaged in an animated conversation with the blond divorcée Allison had met earlier. As she watched, he plucked an hors d'oeuvre from a passing waiter's tray and popped it into the woman's mouth. They both laughed, the blonde clamping a hand over her lips as she tried to contain her mirth.

Allison was staggered by a rush of jealous despair. There was the sort of woman Matt belonged with, a sweet-faced former debutante with the proper number of illustrious ancestors adorning her family tree.

Despite the crowded room, loneliness shattered her heart. Why, oh why, had he walked back into her life? She had been content before; now she would always know what she was missing.

Abruptly anger swept away her depression. She was supposed to be independent! So why was she letting her spirit be broken without even lifting a finger to fight? There were plenty of other men here besides Matthew Wakefield, attractive, intelligent men who could fill the emptiness in her life if she only gave them—and herself—a chance.

Pivoting blindly, she collided with a rock-hard body, and looked up to see a tall, fit man with distinguished graying brown hair. He had an air of refinement, from his superbly tailored tuxedo to the Cartier watch on his wrist. His handsome face was darkly satanic, with the blasé expression of a man in his early forties who has experienced it all.

"Excuse me," Allison blurted as the man reached for her elbow to steady her. She breathed a sigh of relief that her champagne glass had been empty. It would have been embarrassing to dump its contents over this man's impeccable clothing.

"No harm done," he said smoothly. There was a flicker of interest in his anthracite eyes as he swiftly took in her lacy blouse, slender waist, and taffeta skirt. "Where were you off to in such a hurry?"

"I was . . . looking for someone." *And I may just have run smack into him,* she thought, gazing at him critically.

"Then I mustn't keep you."

"Oh, no, it wasn't anything important." She smiled at him graciously. "I don't believe we've been introduced. I'm Allison O'Shea."

"Robert Stockton," he replied, shaking her proffered hand. "I see I'm going to have to come to Regina's parties more often. Her guest list has most definitely acquired a lovely addition." Again, he gave her that admiring look that was a balm to her battered ego.

"Do you know Regina well?" Allison asked.

"I'm a neighbor. And you?"

"I came with . . . a friend."

"Ah, a man, you mean."

"Yes, but I'd rather not talk about him if you don't mind."

"A disagreement, hmm?" Robert observed sagely. "He's a fool to have neglected you, and I'll be happy to help you forget him. Let me get you some more champagne."

He motioned to a servant, who hurried over to refill their glasses. For the next half hour, they chatted with a light, familiar ease. Allison learned that Robert was the publisher of a prominent world news magazine. His conversation was urbane and witty and spiced with compliments.

Once she glanced up and saw that Matt still stood talking to the blond divorcée. His eyes met Allison's; then he looked away, a brooding expression on his face. She redoubled her effort at conversation with Robert, desperate to convince herself that she could overcome the pain that pierced her heart.

When Robert discovered through the course of conversation that she collected old books, he mentioned that their hostess shared her interest. "Why don't I show you Regina's library?" he suggested.

"If you're sure she wouldn't mind."

"Of course she won't."

The library, on the other side of the entrance hall, was furnished with the same stately elegance as the rest of the home. There were ceiling-high bookshelves, two wingback chairs in front of a fireplace, and an Aubusson rug on the floor. The air was cool, and Allison shivered as she set down her champagne glass and walked over to scan the contents of the shelves.

"Cold?" She felt Robert's arm slide around her back, his breath warm on her face.

"Just a little. I'll get used to it in a minute." Allison shrugged off his arm and reached for a book. "Look, here's a first edition of *Sinbad the Sailor*, illustrated by Edmund Dulac. He's one of my favorites. See? Isn't his work gorgeous?"

Robert barely glanced at the opened book. "You're gorgeous," he murmured, nuzzling her neck.

"Robert, please," Allison protested, twisting free.

"Come now," he chided suavely. "I want to kiss you—what's wrong with that?"

What indeed? she wondered with a flash of bitterness. She shouldn't be pining for Matt. Hadn't she learned her lesson about becoming too dependent on him for her happiness? Robert was a handsome, cultured man, so why wasn't she attracted to him? Why were her thoughts always full of Matt—Matt's hands, his mouth, his touch? Why could no man move her as he did?

Robert smiled seductively and drew closer, clearly mistaking her hesitation for shyness. Allison watched him approach, but she couldn't speak. She stood as if paralyzed, the reason for her reluctance now crystal clear in her mind. She would never be able to respond to another man. There would always be something missing. It was that special spark only one man had ever aroused in her. It was love. And whether or not they were together, she would always belong to Matt.

Robert leaned over and captured her mouth with the mastery of long years of practice. With the unfamiliar, unwanted touch of his lips, Allison at last was able to move. With desperate determination, she pushed against his chest, but his only reaction was to tighten his hold. A sensation of sickness was rising in Allison's throat. She finally dragged her lips free, her mind churning with confused despair.

"Robert, please, I—"

She stopped, her eyes widening as she caught sight of a man storming toward them. It was Matt!

He seized Robert and yanked him away from her, flinging him against a row of bookshelves so hard that a small porcelain figurine tumbled to the floor and shattered.

"What the hell's your problem?" Robert demanded.

"I'll tell you what!" Matt snarled, tightening his grip on the other man's shoulders, his face dark with fury. "By God, I ought to kill you for touching her!" He drew back his fist.

Aghast, Allison leaped forward and latched onto his arm. "Don't, Matt! Please!"

Later she wondered how he had heard the almost imperceptible moan over the sound of her voice. But his gaze darted to the doorway.

She followed the direction of his eyes to see Regina Wakefield standing there, swaying, staring at them in horror. In slow motion, the elderly woman collapsed to the floor.

Matt released Robert and rushed to his mother's side. "Oh, my God!" he breathed, gently prying loose the buttons of her high collar.

He threw a swift, urgent glance at the curious crowd gathering outside the library, and barked impatiently, "Someone get Milton Baxter, and fast! She's had a heart attack!"

Chapter Twelve

It took exactly fifteen footsteps to walk the length of Regina Wakefield's library. Allison knew that well, because for the past two hours she had trod that path innumerable times. Six paces to the first wingback chair, three more to the other chair, and six again to the window.

She paused there to stare out into the night. It was snowing in earnest now. The last of the guests had long since departed, and the street was deserted. The glow cast by the front-porch light illuminated the frosting of white on the brick sidewalk. As she watched, a gust of wind flung the thickly falling flakes into a frenzied dance.

Allison swallowed, trying to ease the oppressive heaviness in her chest. It was her fault that the party had ended so abruptly, her fault that Regina Wakefield had fallen ill. Oh, Lord, she'd give anything to undo the evening's tragic chain of events! Why had she gone with Robert to the empty library when he was so obviously interested in her?

Misery filled her heart as she left the window to sink into one of the wingback chairs. It seemed like years instead of just hours had passed since the paramedics, under Milton Baxter's direction, had eased Regina onto a stretcher. She had looked so deathly pale, a pathetic shadow of a woman. Allison had wanted to accompany Matt to the hospital, but he had curtly ordered her to stay put. And she couldn't argue with him, not after what she had done.

Somewhere, a door slammed. Attributing the faint sound to the crew of maids who were cleaning up the party debris, Allison leaned her head back and stared at the ornately plastered ceiling. What if Matt didn't come back tonight? What if he were so disgusted with her that he never wanted to see her again?

Dread squeezed her throat, but she firmly pushed her fears aside. Wasn't Matt a reasonable man? When he had time to think about it, surely he would understand that she hadn't meant for any of the night's events to happen. It had all been a terrible mistake.

Abruptly the library doors opened. Matt stood on the threshold, tall and overwhelmingly masculine in his tuxedo. His face was creased with lines of tiredness. Allison leaped to her feet, her taffeta skirt rustling as she hurried to him.

"I didn't hear you drive up," she exclaimed. "How is your mother? Is she going to be all right?"

"She's fine. It wasn't a heart attack, after all; she'd only fainted."

"I'm so glad," Allison said fervently, feeling a load lift from her mind. "Did you bring her home?"

"No. Milton wanted her to stay overnight for observation."

"Well, at least we can thank God it wasn't anything serious."

Matt stared at her a moment. "Forgive me if I'm a little surprised at your concern," he drawled, his voice mocking. "I was under the impression that you were the type who only cared about yourself."

"How can you say that?" Bewildered hurt banished her relief. "You know that's not true."

"You . . . Oh, forget it. Come on, I'll drive you home." He turned on his heel and strode away.

With a sinking heart, Allison followed him. His expression of contempt had told her that he did, indeed, hold her responsible for his mother's collapse. She couldn't really blame him. If only she hadn't behaved like a stupid fool!

"I'm sorry about tonight," she began awkwardly when they were in his Ferrari, inching down the snow-covered street.

"Oh?"

His skepticism wasn't encouraging, but she went on anyway. "I never meant for things to happen the way they did."

"Is that so?"

"Yes. Matt, you've got to believe me, I—"

"Cut the explanations," he lashed out with sudden savagery. "Haven't you done enough damage for one night without causing me to have an accident, too? I don't want to hear another word out of you until we get home."

Allison clamped her mouth shut, stung by his harshness. Staring blindly into the swirling snowflakes, she sat huddled in her seat, chills running over her skin despite the warmth of her fox jacket. She could understand Matt's need to concentrate on the hazardous road conditions, but why did he have to be so hateful about it?

Once they had crawled onto the highway, where snowplows were already out in full force, Matt drove with barely restrained fury, cutting in and out of lanes with expert control. His hands were tight around the steering wheel, his face taut and grim. Not once did he look in Allison's direction. She might have been a sack of groceries, for all he seemed to care.

It was with an enormous sensation of relief that she finally saw the exit for Copperwood. Tension from the long, silent ride left her shaky. When they walked into the house a short while later, Matt muttered something about needing a drink and headed straight for the kitchen.

Allison let Winston outside. On impulse, she stood on the porch in the cold waiting for the dog, her face tilted up to let the frigid flakes kiss her warm skin. The icy sensation was refreshing, restoring her flagging confidence. She and Matt would work things out. Once he got over his anger, he would understand she had never meant for things to happen the way they had. Granted, she shouldn't have encouraged Robert. But how could she have foreseen that Regina Wakefield would walk in on such an ugly scene?

Winston bounded back to the porch, his paws frosted with white. Allison had to laugh at him; snow never failed to turn her lazy hound into a puppy again.

She felt hopeful as she entered the library. The fresh scent of pine wafted through the air from the Christmas tree in the corner. Matt was standing with his back to her, looking into the cold ashes of the hearth. A bottle of Scotch sat on the mantel. He swung sharply to face her, staring until her tentative smile faded. Without taking his dark gaze from her, he polished off his drink. Then he pivoted to pour another.

"Matt?" She stripped off her fur jacket, draping it over one of the love seats. "We need to talk—"

"You're damn right we do," he snapped.

Stunned by the violence that burned in the depths of his eyes, Allison took an instinctive step backward, a hand rising to her throat, where a pulse beat rapidly beneath her fingertips. The contempt that radiated from him quivered in the air between them.

"Matt, I swear I didn't mean for things to happen the way they did—"

"Then why don't you tell me what in hell you did intend?" he demanded through gritted teeth.

"I . . . I made a mistake—"

"Did you?" he mocked coldly. "Don't forget, I saw the way you and Stockton were kissing. It sure didn't look to me like a mistake—you were enjoying every damned minute of it!" Taking a large swig of Scotch, he paced before the fireplace like a caged panther.

Allison felt a sudden wave of nausea. How could

she make him see the truth? She took a step toward him, holding her hands out in beseechment.

"You misunderstood, Matt. I wasn't kissing Robert. I was trying to push him away from me."

Matt sent her such a dark look of disbelief that her hands shrank back, her arms curling defensively over her breasts.

"My first impulse was to kill the bastard for daring to touch you," he stated coldly. "At the time, it didn't matter whether or not you had invited Stockton's attentions. But in retrospect, I'm glad I was cheated of the chance. Why should I risk a murder rap over a woman who couldn't give a damn about me?" His face twisted in sudden anguish. *"Christ!"*

Abruptly he wheeled, hurling his glass at the fireplace. Pieces shattered over the brick hearth. Gripping the mantel with both hands, he bent his head, his shoulders slumping in defeat. Pain pierced her, and she stepped toward him, stopping just behind him, at a loss for words.

Tell him how wrong he is about the way you feel, her heart urged. *Tell him how much you love him. Tell him . . .*

Instead Allison pleaded, "Matt, you must believe me. I acted stupidly, and I regret it. I never meant to hurt you."

He turned slowly, his face drawn with bitterness. "Yes, you acted stupidly. But the fact remains that in another few minutes I might have intruded on an even more intimate scene."

She gasped at his implication. "How can you say such a thing?"

"Because I know how much you love sex." His

mouth curved into a sardonic smile. "I saw the way you were enjoying his company at the party, and so when you both disappeared, I figured you couldn't wait to be alone with him."

For a split second she was so shocked at his presumption that she was frozen. Then anger boiled within her, burning away the ice until she was seething. Yes, she had acted childishly; but she didn't deserve this sort of treatment!

She flew at him, her hand arcing out to connect with his cheek. The resounding smack of her open palm left a vivid imprint on his skin.

"Get out of my house!" she blazed.

He snared her wrist, jerking her roughly against him. "I'll leave here when I'm good and ready!"

"Take your hands off me!"

"Not until I'm through with you."

With a cry of frustrated fury, Allison tried to spin away. But he held her firmly imprisoned against his warm body. They stared at each other in a battle of wills, and she felt her courage ebb at the grim determination in his eyes.

For some strange reason, she thought he had never looked so handsome, so implacably male. She swallowed and glanced away, her gaze falling to the fingers entrapping her wrist. But that failed to help her regain a righteous anger. All she could think of were those strong hands streaked with crisp black hairs, hands that had once held her with such tenderness, hands that could transport her to paradise.

Her eyes returned to his face. For a fleeting instant she thought she saw a hint of softness there, then decided it was her imagination.

"Do you know what your problem is?" he asked, speaking with far more calm than before.

"No, but I have a feeling you're about to tell me."

He ignored her sarcasm. "Nothing matters to you but your own selfish gratification. You're so damn hung up on being independent that you can't commit yourself to just one man."

"Maybe I don't need a man," she retorted. "I have my family and friends."

"That's safer, isn't it? There's not much risk involved in loving your parents or your sister's kids. You don't get hurt—but the trouble is, you also miss the joys of sharing your life with an equal partner."

"If you're waiting for me to say I need you, then you're going to be disappointed," she taunted, the memory of that long-ago rejection stabbing her heart. "I don't want a permanent man in my life—least of all you!"

There was a flare of pain on his face before all emotion drained away, leaving only bleakness. He thrust her from him so that she stumbled backward onto one of the love seats.

"Live your sterile existence, then," he said with quiet coldness. "I no longer want any part of it."

Pivoting, he walked to the door. A flash of déjà vu seared her suddenly. He was walking out of her life again, only this time it was forever! Panic clogged her throat, and she leaped up to run after him.

"Matt, wait!" she pleaded. "Why can't we go on living together as we have been?"

In the doorway, he paused, staring at the fingers she wound around the finely tailored material of his sleeve. Then he looked at her, bitter sadness on his face.

"Because I've learned something this evening," he said softly. "I've finally gotten it through my thick skull that you'll never love me or marry me. That means we have a dead-end relationship."

Matt walked away and mounted the stairs. Too numb to move or even think, Allison leaned her forehead against the door frame. Her heart lurched in faint hope as she heard his footsteps descending to the foyer a short while later. But seeing the suitcase in his hand was like feeling a knife slash her soul. Without saying a word, he strode to the front door and wrenched it open.

"Matt, please . . ." she began, torn asunder at the prospect of losing him, yet even more scared to trust him.

But this time he didn't stop. The door slammed shut behind him, causing the Christmas wreath on the back of it to sway, then slowly come to a halt.

Allison shivered, and she knew it was from more than just the draft of icy air from outside. She was gripped by a chill that penetrated her very core.

The sound of the Ferrari roaring out of the driveway died in the distance, and silence settled over her like a shroud.

Chapter Thirteen

*H*alls decked with holly. Jingling bells. Chestnuts roasting over a roaring fire. Red-nosed people rushing from store to store to buy last-minute gifts.

It was the morning of Christmas Eve, and Allison lay in bed, trying to coax herself into a holiday spirit. But no matter how hard she tried, she couldn't shake the starkness in her heart. She yearned for Matt, wanting the security of him stretched out beside her, warm and loving . . .

Her hand stroked over the empty pillow next to her. All she had left to keep her company in this rambling old house were her pets. At one time, that would have satisfied her. But now it was scant comfort to see Winston and Esmerelda curled up at the foot of the bed when she had lost the only man she had ever loved.

226

Though she had gone into the relationship with her eyes wide open, knowing that Matt might leave her, what she hadn't anticipated was that his second rejection would be even more cataclysmic than the first. At seventeen, she had loved with an innocence and sweetness; this time, she had experienced all the passion and fire of a mature woman.

Allison stared out the unshaded windows into the frosty gray dawn. She could go after him and try again to explain, but what good would that do? There had been such cold finality in his voice. Could she blame him for hating her, when he had no knowledge of her true feelings? Yet even if they reconciled, how could she trust him not to walk out on her again someday?

Matt was gone for good. Now, after four days, it was time to accept the awful reality. The numbness was wearing off, and pain was setting up permanent residence in her heart. Tears tightened her throat, but she swallowed hard to keep them from spilling over. She had done far too much crying already.

Allison crawled out from under the thick patchwork quilt, welcoming the shock as her bare feet hit the icy pine floor. At least the sensation made her feel a little bit alive.

Take it a day at a time, she advised herself, listlessly dragging on wool slacks. She rooted around in the closet for her favorite sweater, thinking that wearing it might help cheer her up. Separating the hangers of clothing, she froze, staring at a pale-blue shirt that Matt had forgotten. In slow motion, she drew it out and buried her face in its fine texture, inhaling the faint male scent that clung to the fabric.

Oh, why couldn't she stop aching so? Fighting tears, Allison balled up the shirt and shoved it into the darkest corner of the closet. Then she found her sweater and tugged it on over her chilled body.

Winston and Esmerelda trailed her down the stairs, waiting expectantly outside the kitchen door for their breakfast. Mechanically Allison put their food bowls out in the hall, then fed Mr. Screech, Louisa, the kittens, and her fish.

Nothing appealed to her own stomach but hot coffee. While it perked, she reached into the cabinet for a mug. She had it in her hands when the sudden ringing of the telephone jarred her shattered nerves. The mug slipped from her fingers and smashed on the brick floor. Pieces scattered everywhere, but thankfully none struck any of the kittens.

Allison made an involuntary move to clean up the shards, but the jangle of the telephone stopped her. Lord, she was losing her mind to forget so quickly what had made her drop the mug in the first place! Carefully wending her way through the mess, she picked up the receiver.

"Hello?"

"Hello, Allison?" The regal voice had a slight quaver. "This is Regina Wakefield."

Allison stiffened with shock. Of all the people in the world who might have called, Matt's mother was the last she would have suspected! Her fingers tightened around the phone, her mouth too stunned to form words.

"Allison, are you there?"

She took a deep breath. "How are you, Mrs. Wakefield? I . . . I hope you're feeling better."

"I am, thank you."

"Are you out of the hospital, then?"

"Yes, I'm home again." There was a slight hesitation. "I know this is rather spur-of-the-moment, but I wondered if I might possibly persuade you to come here for lunch at noon today?"

The invitation was as unexpected as the phone call. Questions raced through Allison's mind. Why would Regina Wakefield want to see her? Had she not heard that Matt had broken things off? Did she want to warn Allison to stay away from her son?

"I don't know if I can make it—"

"Oh, please do try." Regina Wakefield's voice took on a note of urgency. "I . . . I really need to talk to you."

Allison opened her mouth to refuse but somehow an acceptance popped out instead. "All right, I'll be there."

You're a glutton for punishment, Allison thought, hearing a distant church bell toll the hour of noon as she mounted the granite steps to Regina Wakefield's Beacon Hill home. She had been telling herself that all morning, yet she had found herself changing into a soft-rose wool dress, disguising the circles under her eyes with makeup, and driving into Boston. She had arrived thirty minutes early, and had spent the time parked near Louisburg Square, wondering which of the beautiful old houses there belonged to Matt. She had even half-hoped she might see him, but fate had not been on her side.

Now, as her hand hesitated over the brass door-knocker, Allison fought a cowardly urge to turn and run. What had induced her to come here anyway? Curiosity? Yes, a little, she admitted. But maybe there was a more compelling motivation. Maybe deep down she harbored a crazy hope that somehow she might convince Regina Wakefield that she really was good enough for Matt. Not, of course, that that would make much difference now, but it might be a psychological victory when she needed so badly to perk up her spirits.

Allison gave three firm raps on the door, hearing the sound echo in the foyer beyond. A servant opened the door and took her coat, then led her into the library, where Regina Wakefield sat, her thin body swallowed by one of the wingback chairs.

"Hello, Mrs. Wakefield."

"Please, call me Regina," she said as she rose, an oddly uncertain quality to her smile. "I'm so glad you could come."

"Thank you for inviting me, Regina," Allison recited dutifully. She shook the woman's hand. It felt fragile, like paper skin stretched over bird bones and blue veins.

"Could I get you something to drink before we eat? A glass of wine, perhaps?"

"No, thank you," Allison refused politely. She wanted to have a clear head for this encounter.

Regina touched the strand of pearls at her throat in an almost nervous gesture. "Oh . . . well, then, I believe lunch is ready, if you would come with me. The kitchen and dining area are on the second floor."

They went out into the foyer, where the air was filled with a pine scent from the Christmas tree in the drawing room. Holding onto the mahogany balustrade, Regina started up the elegant curving staircase. Her steps were slow, as if each move had to be carefully orchestrated lest her frail body fail her with a slip of the foot. The regal-blue dress she wore with its expertly cut folds of fabric failed to disguise the near gauntness of her figure. But her spine was still erect and her head held high, as if she were determined not to invite pity.

Allison's heart softened. Despite her wariness, she couldn't help admiring Regina's spirit. Something compelled her to stay protectively close to the elderly woman. Regina smiled, noticing her concern.

"I'm really not as breakable as I look."

"Wouldn't it be better if you had an elevator installed?"

"There is one at the rear of the house which I use sometimes, but Milton is adamant about my exercising whenever possible."

At the second floor, Regina led her down a hall past a formal dining room containing a long polished table, and into a more cozy, inviting room. The atmosphere here was like an old-fashioned boudoir. The room was decorated in yellow chintz, with two plump chairs in front of a white marble fireplace. With a stab of pain, Allison saw a photograph of Matt on the mantel. She looked away, aware of a sudden lump in her throat.

"This is my sitting room," Regina said, directing her to a small, linen-draped table near the window. "I often have my meals here when I'm alone. I . . . I thought that since it was just the two of us, it might be more comfortable." Again, there was that slight hesitation in her voice, as if she were uncertain of something.

"It's lovely," Allison gently assured her.

"Thank you. Please, make yourself at home, while I tell the cook we're ready."

As Regina left the room, Allison took a seat at the table. Thoughtfully she stared down at the china plate with its thin gold border. It was startling to realize that she didn't feel as intimidated by Matt's mother as she had in the past. A memory flashed through her mind of those stark, formal meals with his parents back when she had been an awkward seventeen-year-old. Compared to her own outgoing parents, Matt's mother had been reserved, distant, proper. But now, Allison wondered if she might have misjudged the woman. Was Regina really so haughty and cold? Could it be that she had only seemed that way due to an innate shyness?

That suspicion grew stronger through lunch. A young maid in an aproned uniform served each course. There was homemade mushroom soup, a spinach salad, and filet of sole in a delicate cream sauce. Allison tried to do the meal justice, though she'd had little appetite for the past few days. As they chatted idly about Copperwood, where the Wakefields had once lived, she realized that she was seeing Matt's mother through the eyes of an adult. She wondered again what Regina wanted to talk to her about. Whatever it was, the older woman didn't seem to be in any hurry to bring it up.

Afterward, they sat in the yellow chintz chairs in front of the hearth, where a fire crackled cheerfully.

Regina dismissed the hovering maid and poured the coffee herself. She handed a cup to Allison, setting the silver pot on a cherrywood table.

"I suppose you've been wondering why I asked you to come here today on such short notice." Regina paused, raising a nervous hand to her pearls. "First of all, I . . . I wanted to apologize for fainting at the party. I didn't mean to ruin everyone's evening."

"But there's no need to apologize," Allison exclaimed. "You'd had a bad shock, walking in on that scene. No, if anyone is at fault, it's me. I was the real cause . . ." She stopped, biting her lip, wondering if Regina had heard Matt's twisted version of the story.

"My son wouldn't tell me the details of what happened, and I didn't want to press him," the older woman commented gently.

Allison hesitated. "It was just that . . . he found another man kissing me," she said awkwardly. "He didn't realize I was trying to resist—after all, I had left the party with Robert. I never thought Matt would react with such violence."

Regina's face was inscrutable. "Surely you explained things to him later."

"Of course, but he didn't believe me." With a heavy sigh, she set her cup on a table, having lost interest in the coffee.

"So that's why you and he are no longer living together?"

Allison's head shot up in surprise. "You knew he'd moved in with me?"

"Yes, Matthew had told me."

"And you didn't object?"

"Object?" Regina shrugged. "It was not, perhaps, the sort of arrangement I would have wished for, but then Matthew is a grown man. I no longer have the right to tell him what to do."

"No, I suppose not." Silently Allison added, *But I'm sure you'd rather he date someone in his own social circle, a woman like that blond divorcée.*

"I knew that something had been deeply troubling my son ever since Saturday night," Regina went on, putting her coffee cup aside to fidget with her pearls. "Yesterday evening I persuaded him to come here for dinner, and managed to drag it out of him that he was no longer seeing you. But he refused to discuss it further." She tried to smile, but there was too much pain in her eyes. "I was so afraid that I had again stirred up trouble between the two of you."

"None of this was your fault," Allison reassured her, a little puzzled by the elderly woman's distress. Why would it matter to Regina who was to blame so long as it kept Matt from marrying beneath his social class? "Besides," she added with false nonchalance, "it was inevitable that Matt and I would split up sometime. That scene Saturday night only brought things out into the open."

Regina looked confused. "Why do you say inevitable?"

"Matt was bound to lose interest in me sooner or later."

"But he loves you."

"I know that's what he says. Unfortunately that wasn't enough to hold us together once, so why should it be now?"

Regina was still frowning. "But twelve years ago there were extenuating circumstances which made him believe he had no other choice than to break off your engagement."

"Yes, how could I forget?" Allison said bitterly, remembering his excuses about financial problems when it was really a case of his not loving her enough to defy his parents. She stiffened her spine, fingers digging into her soft wool skirt. "Look, Regina, there's no point in discussing this any further. I know you don't want your son to marry me, and I can assure you there's nothing for you to worry about. It's highly unlikely that he and I will ever get back together again."

Regina's expression of bewilderment deepened. "But I don't oppose a marriage between you and Matthew. I'm very much in favor of it."

Allison stared in astonishment. "I don't understand . . ."

"What else would have induced me to meddle so in my son's life by asking you here like this? If there were even a chance that I had somehow caused trouble between you two again, I wanted to try to rectify the situation."

"Then you admit that you did cause our breakup twelve years ago?"

"Indirectly, yes."

"Indirectly!" Allison shook her head in sudden anger. "You and your husband convinced Matt to stop seeing me!"

An expression of hurt crept over Regina's wrinkled face. "How can you blame me for having a heart attack?"

"Heart attack?" Allison repeated blankly.

"You didn't know? But I thought you said Matthew had told you—"

"He told me about the financial problems, yes."

"But that's only half the story, and the least important half at that. I can scarcely believe he would expect you to understand, yet not explain . . ."

Regina sighed, staring into the fire, her eyes both thoughtful and troubled. She absently touched the pearls at her throat, then looked at Allison.

"I must tell you this, not because I wish to interfere, but because you have a right to know." She paused. "Perhaps it's best to start by saying that Matthew and I have always been very close. My late husband and I had longed for a family, but after fifteen years of marriage we had given up hope. One of the happiest days of my life was the day I found out I was pregnant." Regina smiled, lost in memories. "I was forty years old when Matthew was born. I admit we were indulgent, possessive, doting parents, but we also demanded that Matthew give us his best in return.

"The summer he turned eighteen, my husband and I went off to Europe on a long-awaited vacation, leaving Matthew behind with my sister-in-law in Copperwood. That's when you and he met. When we returned in September, I found out by accident about the financial problems Wakefield Mills was having. I was furious with my husband. Why had we wasted so much money on a trip? Why hadn't we stayed in Boston so he could work on finding solutions to the problems?"

A sad expression stole across Regina's face.

"Much as I loved him, my husband was never much of a businessman. Anyway, the point is that I was already under considerable strain, so when Matthew came home one night and announced he intended to marry you, we got into a terrible fight. I told him about the financial problems, that he was too young for marriage and was only rebelling. I'm ashamed to admit, I also accused him of not loving me. I realize now that I was jealous." Her voice was filled with self-reproach. "For so long, I'd been the only woman in his life.

"In the middle of our argument, I began having chest pains. Matthew and my husband rushed me to the hospital, and it was a good thing, because I'd suffered a heart attack. For weeks afterward my son refused to discuss the engagement. Finally I dragged it out of him that he was no longer seeing you. I decided not to interfere, convincing myself that I was doing what was best for him."

Regina stared into the fire, her face tormented. "It was only much later that I realized I had underestimated the depth of his feelings. Granted, you were both too young, but my son had broken up with you for all the wrong reasons. He had done it out of a misplaced guilt, thinking his relationship with you had caused my heart attack. He refused to see that I had already been under a tremendous strain due to our finances."

Allison sat in stunned silence, her fingers curled into fists. Yes, she could understand Matt's guilt. Wouldn't she have reacted the same way under similar circumstances?

Regina's voice quavered as she added, "How many times I've berated myself for acting so stupidly! Through my own selfishness, I'd destroyed Matthew's life. He buried himself in his work and, on the rare occasions when he dated, it was a different woman every time. He had no interest in developing any close relationships.

"I urged him to reconcile with you. I tried to tell him that my heart attack had not been his fault, but he refused to listen. We argued, and he ended up moving out. Then one day not too long ago he told me he intended to see you. Can you imagine how happy that made me? At last there was a chance that the mistakes of the past would be rectified, that my son would find happiness again. Then yesterday evening he told me it was over. After what had happened on Saturday night, I feared I might be the cause once again, but this time I had to do something. That's why I invited you here today."

Regina fell silent, and Allison sprang up from her chair, absently massaging the soft wool covering her arms. She paced over to the fireplace, trying to assimilate what she had just heard. What a heavy burden of guilt for Matt to bear, to think he'd caused his mother's heart attack! That much she could accept. Yet there were so many unanswered questions.

"If you really wanted Matt and me to reconcile, then why did you say earlier that you'd rather we didn't live together?"

"All I meant was that I'd prefer for you two to get married first. I suppose I'm a little conventional in that respect."

"But what about Milton Baxter? He warned me to stay clear of Matt for your sake."

"Are you sure?" Regina said with a frown. "What exactly did he say to you?"

"Something about not wanting to see you distressed because of your health."

"But of course he must have meant that I would be upset if you and my son were to separate again."

Allison leaned a weak shoulder against the fireplace mantel, her eyes straying to the photo of Matt. Was it possible that she had misinterpreted things so drastically?

"And you really don't mind that I'm Irish Catholic and come from a lower class background than you do?" she asked.

Regina smiled. "My grandfather was an immigrant Englishman, a bricklayer. His wife, my grandmother, was a seamstress. They were both wonderful people, and I wouldn't have traded them for all the world. What matters is not where you come from but what you make of yourself." Her eyes turned troubled, her fingers plucking nervously at the chair arm. "I only hope you can forgive me for being so resentful of you. I've caused both you and Matthew so much unhappiness."

Allison left the fireplace to kneel beside the older woman, taking Regina's hand in hers. "There's no need to apologize." Impulsively she added, "And I hope we'll be friends from now on."

Regina smiled. "I would like that very much."

Allison rose to sit on the edge of her chair. Why hadn't Matt told her the real reason he had broken off their engagement? Was it because he'd felt he alone was to blame for his mother's heart attack? Or maybe it was her own fault, she reflected guiltily.

After all, every time he'd mentioned his parents, she had exploded with anger. Perhaps he'd decided it was best to steer clear of the topic.

Regina leaned forward with an earnest expression. "At the risk of meddling more than I already have, may I ask what you'll do now? Will you try to talk to my son again and work things out?"

Allison bit her lip. "I . . . I don't know, Regina. I didn't show much faith in him. He might not even want me back now."

"He's been wrong, too," Regina pointed out. "For one, he didn't tell you about my heart attack."

"That's true, but . . . maybe I've become too independent for marriage."

"How do you know whether or not it'll work unless you try?" Regina said quietly. "Do you really love my son?"

"Yes."

"And have you told him so?"

"No," Allison admitted with a reluctant shake of her head.

"Then don't you think you owe it to the both of you to at least let him know how you feel? You have so much to gain, and what can you lose but a little pride?"

Regina's words were so like Colleen's. *You have to be willing to take a chance when you love someone.* Could she take that step and trust Matt? And could she give up her independence? Allison searched her soul and, for the first time, found that her need for him transcended all else. In a flash of insight, she realized that love would enhance her life rather than limit it.

She surged up from the chair and on impulse

threw her arms around Regina, kissing the elderly woman's cheek. "Thank you for helping me see how foolish I've been."

"Then you'll speak to him?"

"I'll try." Allison felt her heart twist with vulnerability. What if Matt didn't want her? "I only hope it's not too late, because otherwise it won't be a very merry Christmas."

Regina's eyes glistened with moisture. "I'll be praying, then, that you have the happiest Christmas of your life."

Chapter Fourteen

$\mathscr{D}$ usk was spreading deep shadows in the surrounding woods as Allison guided her BMW over the bumpy road that led to the textile mill. Reluctant to talk to Matt by telephone, she had gotten his Beacon Hill address from Regina, and had gone to his house in Louisburg Square in the hopes of finding him there. But he hadn't been home. Next, she had tried the Wakefield Mills corporate headquarters building in downtown Boston, but again she had had no success. No one in his plush executive offices seemed to be sure exactly where he was.

So she had left the slush and traffic of the city and headed back to Copperwood, intending to check the mill. A sudden inspiration made her stop at home first before resuming her search. There, she had quickly wrapped a gift for him; now a large red-and-green package rested on the front seat beside her. It made sense that Matt would be at the mill, she thought as she bumped over the potholes in the road. It was just like him to be working even though it was Christmas Eve.

Up ahead, the chain-link fence that marked the boundary of the mill property stretched off through the barren trees. At the sound of her car, a young man in uniform stepped out of the small guardhouse and swung open the gate. Allison identified his lanky form. Rob Morgan. The last time she had seen him he had been unemployed, but now it appeared that Matt had hired him. She felt a surge of guilt, remembering how she had accused Matt of leading Rob on with false promises of a job.

She drove inside and braked to a stop, rolling down her window and shivering as cold air rushed into her car. "Hi, Rob! I didn't know you were working here now."

"Yeah, it's been about a week since I started. Let me tell you, the money sure is going to come in handy."

"I'm glad to hear it," Allison said sincerely. "Say, can you tell me if Matt's still here?"

"He sure is. The boss told everyone to go home a couple of hours ago, but I thought I'd hang around for a little while and watch the place till he left. But now I'm beginning to wonder how long he plans on staying. If I stick around much longer, I'll miss having dinner with my kids."

"Well, maybe I'll be able to talk him into leaving."

"I hope so. Nobody ought to be working on Christmas Eve."

"Then follow your own advice and head home,"

Allison said with a laugh. "And merry Christmas! Tell your grandmother I send my best."

"Sure will. Merry Christmas to you, too."

Rob waved as she drove on. Allison cranked up her window in a hurry to keep the icy air out. Pulling into the parking lot, empty but for Matt's truck, she turned off the engine. The lavender tint in the western sky was fading fast. Night was busily laying thick shadows in the tangled woods that surrounded the complex. The river was a faint glimmer in the distance, its edge marked by spikes of dead brown reeds. The big mill looked dark and deserted. She could see no light in the smaller structure off to the right, either, but knew that that was because Matt's office was around the corner.

Taking a deep breath for courage, Allison left the car, the gift in her hands. Her breath condensed in the frosty air as she carefully maneuvered her high heels over the ice patches on the cracked concrete pavement. A gust of frigid wind whipped around her exposed legs, making her regret not changing out of the rose wool dress into warm slacks. She tensed her muscles against the bitter cold.

Yet, eager as she was to escape the chilly air, her fingers hesitated on the doorknob to the building housing his office. Panic jarred her nerves. What if he rejected her? She tried to concentrate on what Regina had said, that all she had to lose was her pride. But Allison knew there was more at stake than just that. Now she had her hopes up, and to have them crushed would also crush her heart.

She swallowed hard and wrested open the door, walking down the dim hall and into the darkened outer office. The desk here was neat, the chair empty, a plastic cover concealing the electric typewriter. Her footsteps were silent on the thick carpeting as she headed toward the slender chink of light emanating from the room beyond.

Allison peeked in the partly open door, knowing she was delaying the moment of reckoning yet unable to help herself. From her limited viewpoint, she couldn't see his desk, but the round conference table in the corner was littered with papers and ashtrays filled with cigarette butts. Carelessly tossed over a chair was a navy suitcoat, along with a tie. And there, one shoulder slumped against the window frame, was Matt.

He was staring out into the dusk, his back to her. The sleeves of his white shirt were rolled up his muscled forearms to just shy of his elbows. His normally neat black hair was rumpled, as though he'd run his fingers through it innumerable times. He held a cigarette and, as she watched, he took a long drag on it.

Something in his slouching posture made her heart turn over. Was there really dejection in the slant of those broad shoulders, or was she just imagining it? Could it be he was thinking about her, and wishing, as she wished, that they might find a way to settle their differences once and for all?

Don't get your hopes up too much. Don't forget, he told you he wanted no part of your life anymore.

A reluctant push of her hand opened the door. Though she was quiet, Matt must have seen the movement reflected in the window glass, because he swung to face her. She saw something she couldn't identify flash across his features, then swiftly his shoulders straightened and all emotion vanished from those deep amber eyes.

"Hello, Matt," she said, her voice soft and hesitant.

"Allison." He acknowledged her presence with a tilt of his head, not giving her even a flicker of encouragement.

She took a tentative step into the room. "I brought you a Christmas present." She indicated the brightly wrapped box cradled in the crook of her arm.

"How very civilized," he commented. "The ex-lovers exchanging Christmas gifts after the affair is over."

Allison winced inside at his mocking tone. Pasting on a smile, she crossed to the conference table and put the package down, then removed her coat and draped it over a chair, trying to bolster her courage.

"Matt, the gift was only an excuse to come here."

"And why would you want to see me?" He casually stubbed out his cigarette in an overflowing ashtray. "If you're looking for another quick roll in the hay, count me out. I'm not interested."

That hurt. But she couldn't blame him for being bitter. It was her own fault for letting him believe that she didn't love him.

"That's not why I'm here," she forced herself to go on. "I . . . only want to talk."

"Do you? I wonder why? So you can tell me again how much you want my body? Well, it won't work, Allison, because I'm through being used. If you need sex, you'll just have to find yourself another stud. I'm not available."

"You've got this all wrong." She crossed her arms and took a deep breath. "I came here to say that I'd made a mistake in not trusting you. Matt, why didn't you tell me about your mother's heart attack? It would have helped me understand why you felt compelled to end our engagement."

He picked up a sheet of paper from the table and glanced at it, hiding the expression in his eyes. "I take it you've been talking to my mother."

"I had lunch with her today, and she inadvertently let it slip. Why, Matt? Why didn't you just tell me the truth?"

He tossed the piece of paper back onto the table and looked at her. "There was no point in laying that guilt on you."

"But you weren't responsible for what happened. Your mother said it was the financial strain that was the primary cause of her heart attack, not our relationship."

"I know that now. I wouldn't have come back to you otherwise."

"Then what was the problem? Why couldn't you have told me?"

"I meant to eventually, but the time never seemed right." He paused for a moment's reflection. "Maybe, too, I never got rid of a gut-level feeling of responsibility. Rationally I could accept what my mother said, but emotionally I couldn't."

"Oh, Matt, you should have been honest with me. It really *would* have helped me understand."

He shrugged. "But I'd already admitted I'd made a mistake when I broke our engagement, that maybe things would have been different if I'd have been more mature. That should have been enough to convince you to put the past behind us."

Allison took a step toward him. "But don't you see? Since you'd left me once on a flimsy excuse, I was afraid you might run out on me again if the going got rough."

"Maybe you should have trusted me," he said bitterly.

"Maybe so," she conceded. "But trust is a two-way street. Why didn't you believe *me* when I tried to tell you there was nothing between me and Robert Stockton?"

"Should I have?"

"Yes."

He stared at her, then gave a heavy sigh and ran a hand through his hair. "I guess that night I was already angry because our relationship seemed to be going nowhere. Maybe I was jumping on any excuse to convince myself that you weren't worth the effort."

"I was doing the same thing," Allison admitted softly. "That's why I turned to Robert in the first place—because I saw you across the room talking to that blonde. I was jealous because she had all the breeding and background that I didn't have, so I tried to tell myself that I didn't need you."

Matt frowned. "What blonde?"

"The one who looked like a debutante. You know, she'd just gotten divorced and was going around announcing it to the world."

"Oh, you mean Carol!" He laughed. "I grew up with her. She's like a sister to me."

"She wasn't acting very sisterly. At least that's not the way it looked to me."

"That's just Carol. She's a born flirt." There was a pause, then he added, "But even if she had been romantically interested in me, it wouldn't have done her any good."

Their eyes locked. If Matt was saying he'd had no interest in other women, that incident, Allison reminded herself, had happened before their final breakup. What really mattered was whether or not he felt the same now. *Take the risk . . .*

"Matt, I . . . made a lot of mistakes," she said, her voice uncertain. "Could you ever find it in your heart to forgive me? Could we start over again, without all the lies and mistrust?"

Her eyes pleaded with him. She knew that all it would take was one word, one indication from him that he felt the same as she did, and she'd throw herself into his arms. Her heart plummeted when he abruptly turned his back, propping a hand on the window frame as he stared out the darkened glass.

"I'm sorry, Allison, but you ask the impossible."

"Why?" she choked out. "Why can't you forgive me?"

"It's not the forgiveness I have a problem with, it's the idea of starting over." His voice was tormented, and he didn't look at her. "I simply can't let myself get involved in another dead-end affair with you. What would be the point?"

She stepped forward and put a hand on his arm, feeling his warm, vital flesh beneath her fingertips. "The point is that my life is empty without you there to share it with." Her courage faltered. Now she had to say it. She'd have to say the words that she'd thought she'd never be able to utter again. After a slight hesitation she managed to add softly, "I love you, Matt."

He jerked around to search her face. "Do you really mean that?" he said, his tone low and intent.

"With all my heart."

"Allison." Her name came out in a groan as he pulled her into his strong embrace. Her arms went around his waist, and she tucked her face in his neck, breathing in his familiar scent. Happiness soared within her. He did still want her! For a long moment, they stood there, molded as tightly as if they were one body from head to toe.

"You don't know how long I've waited to hear you say those words," he murmured. "I'd almost given up hoping."

Allison ran her fingers over the slightly abrasive skin of his jaw. "I'm planning on saying it so much, you'll probably get bored hearing me. I love you, I love you, I love you."

He grinned. "So far, I'm not bored in the least."

Their mouths blended in a kiss so sweet and lingering it said more than mere words ever could. It was a poignant experience that transcended the physical. Their hearts and souls were one, with no barriers to separate them.

Blissful minutes passed before she broke away to fetch his Christmas gift from the conference table. Matt tore off the wrapping paper and opened the box. Allison grinned at his surprise when he pulled forth a small stuffed doll of Kit with the parrot Kaboodle perched on her shoulder.

"Remember that licensing offer?" she asked.

"How could I forget?" he groaned.

"This is just my way of saying that what's mine is

now yours too. It's sort of a symbol of my willingness to take the risk of sharing everything I have with you." She looped her arms around his neck. "And you know what? I've decided to take pity on poor old Stanley and let him marry Kit no matter what Kaboodle thinks."

"But that will change the whole focus of the comic strip."

"It's about time Kit learns not to be afraid of marriage. After all, I did."

With a sudden frown, Matt tossed the doll onto the desk and tightened his grip on her. "What are you saying, Allison?" he asked softly.

She met his gaze steadily, hoping that he would see the certainty in her eyes. "I'm saying I want to marry you, Matt."

He searched her face as if afraid to believe what he found there. "We don't have to get married if that's not what you really want," he said. "It's enough to know you love me."

"But it's not enough for me." Emotion flooded her as she reached up and touched his cheek. "I want you to be a permanent part of my life, Matt, now and forever."

His eyes softened. "No regrets?"

"Not a one."

"And you won't mind losing your independence?"

Her lips tilted into a loving smile. "How can I lose when I'm gaining so very, very much?"

ENTER:

Here's your chance to win a fabulous $50,000 diamond jewelry collection, consisting of diamond necklace, bracelet, earrings and ring.

All you have to do to enter is fill out the coupon below and mail it by September 30, 1985.

Send entries to:

In the U.S.	Silhouette Diamond Sweepstakes P.O. Box 779 Madison Square Station New York, NY 10159
In Canada	Silhouette Diamond Sweepstakes Suite 191 238 Davenport Road Toronto, Ontario M5R 1J6

NAME_____

ADDRESS_____

CITY_____ STATE/(PROV.)_____

ZIP/(POSTAL CODE)_____

BCD-A-1

RULES FOR SILHOUETTE DIAMOND SWEEPSTAKES

OFFICIAL RULES—NO PURCHASE NECESSARY

1. Silhouette Diamond Sweepstakes is open to Canadian (except Quebec) and United States residents 18 years or older at the time of entry. Employees and immediate families of the publishers of Silhouette, their affiliates, retailers, distributors, printers, agencies and RONALD SMILEY INC. are excluded.

2. To enter, print your name and address on the official entry form or on a 3" x 5" slip of paper. You may enter as often as you choose, but each envelope must contain only one entry. Mail entries first class in Canada to Silhouette Diamond Sweepstakes, Suite 191, 238 Davenport Road, Toronto, Ontario M5R 1J6. In the United States, mail to Silhouette Diamond Sweepstakes, P.O. Box 779, Madison Square Station, New York, NY 10159. Entries must be postmarked between February 1 and September 30, 1985. Silhouette is not responsible for lost, late or misdirected mail.

3. First Prize of diamond jewelry, consisting of a necklace, ring, bracelet and earrings will be awarded. Approximate retail value is $50,000 U.S./$62,500 Canadian. Second Prize of 100 Silhouette Home Reader Service Subscriptions will be awarded. Approximate retail value of each is $162.00 U.S./$180.00 Canadian. No substitution, duplication, cash redemption or transfer of prizes will be permitted. Odds of winning depend upon the number of valid entries received. One prize to a family or household. Income taxes, other taxes and insurance on First Prize are the sole responsibility of the winners.

4. Winners will be selected under the supervision of RONALD SMILEY INC., an independent judging organization whose decisions are final, by random drawings from valid entries postmarked by September 30, 1985, and received no later than October 7, 1985. Entry in this sweepstakes indicates your awareness of the Official Rules. Winners who are residents of Canada must answer correctly a time-related arithmetical skill-testing question to qualify. First Prize winner will be notified by certified mail and must submit an Affidavit of Compliance within 10 days of notification. Returned Affidavits or prizes that are refused or undeliverable will result in alternative names being randomly drawn. Winners may be asked for use of their name and photo at no additional compensation.

5. For a First Prize winner list, send a stamped self-addressed envelope postmarked by September 30, 1985. In Canada, mail to Silhouette Diamond Contest Winner, Suite 309, 238 Davenport Road, Toronto, Ontario M5R 1J6. In the United States, mail to Silhouette Diamond Contest Winner, P.O. Box 182, Bowling Green Station, New York, NY 10274. This offer will appear in Silhouette publications and at participating retailers. Offer void in Quebec and subject to all Federal, Provincial, State and Municipal laws and regulations and wherever prohibited or restricted by law.

SDR-A-1

MAIL THIS COUPON
and get 4 thrilling
Silhouette Desire®
novels FREE (a $7.80 value)

Silhouette Desire books may not be for everyone. They *are* for readers who want a sensual, provocative romance. These are modern love stories that are charged with emotion from the first page to the thrilling happy ending—about women who discover the extremes of fiery passion. Confident women who face the challenge of today's world and overcome all obstacles to attain their dreams—*and their desires.*

We believe you'll be so delighted with Silhouette Desire romance novels that you'll want to receive them regularly through our home subscription service. Your books will be *shipped to you two months before they're available anywhere else*—so you'll never miss a new title. Each month we'll send you 6 new books to look over for 15 days, without obligation. If not delighted, simply return them and owe nothing. Or keep them and pay only $1.95 each. There's no charge for postage or handling. And there's no obligation to buy anything at any time. You'll also receive a subscription to the Silhouette Books Newsletter *absolutely free!*

So don't wait. To receive your four FREE books, fill out and mail the coupon below *today!*

SILHOUETTE DESIRE and colophon are registered trademarks and a service mark.

Silhouette Desire,® 120 Brighton Road, P.O. Box 5084, Clifton, N.J. 07015-5084

Yes, please send me FREE and without obligation, 4 exciting Silhouette Desire books. Unless you hear from me after I receive them, send me 6 new Silhouette Desire books to preview each month before they're available anywhere else. I understand that you will bill me just $1.95 each for a total of $11.70—with no additional shipping, handling or other hidden charges. **There is no minimum number of books that I must buy, and I can cancel anytime I wish.** The first 4 books are mine to keep, even if I never take a single additional book.

☐ Mrs. ☐ Miss ☐ Ms. ☐ Mr.   BDS2R5

Name	*(please print)*	
Address		Apt. #
City	State	Zip
( ) Area Code	Telephone Number	

Signature (If under 18, parent or guardian must sign.)

This offer limited to one per customer. Terms and prices subject to change. Your enrollment is subject to acceptance by Silhouette Books.

D-OP-A